I DON'T DO MOUNTAINS!

First published in 2024 by Scottish Mountaineering Press.

Copyright © Barbara Henderson.

The author has asserted their rights under the Copyright, Design and Patents Act 1988 to be identified as the authors of this work.

A catalogue record of this book is available from the British Library.

ISBN: 978-1-907233-54-8

All rights reserved. No part of this publication may be reproduced, stored in or introduced into a retrieval system, or transmitted in any form or by any means (electronic, mechanical, photocopying, recording or otherwise), without the prior written permission of the publisher.

This is a work of fiction. Names, characters, places, and incidents either are products of the author's imagination or are used fictitiously. Any resemblance to actual persons, living or dead, events, or locales is entirely coincidental.

Edited by Helen Sedgwick.
Designed by Gino Di Meo Studio.
Illustrated by Victoria Di Meo.

Printed by Bell & Bain
in the United Kingdom.

I DON'T DO MOUNTAINS!

Barbara Henderson

CHAPTER 1
The Announcement
Page 8

CHAPTER 2
Hostile Habitats
Page 13

CHAPTER 3
More than a Match
Page 18

CHAPTER 4
Departure
Page 25

CHAPTER 7
A Home in the Hills
Page 48

CHAPTER 5
Into the Wild
Page 32

CHAPTER 8
Am Fear Liath Mòr
Page 54

CHAPTER 6
Opinions
Page 40

CHAPTER 9
The Morning After
Page 59

CHAPTER 10
War Council
Page 63

CHAPTER 11
An Uneasy Alliance
Page 68

CHAPTER 12
Stuck
75

CHAPTER 13
Night Wandering
Page 81

CHAPTER 14
The Cold Glint of Metal
Page 90

CHAPTER 15
Of Earth and Sky
Page 96

CHAPTER 16
Sorley's Secret
Page 103

CHAPTER 17
Truce
Page 108

CHAPTER 18
The Old Man
Page 115

CHAPTER 19
The Hunting Lodge
Page 123

CHAPTER 20
The Pursuit
Page 129

CHAPTER 21
The Search
Page 133

CHAPTER 22
The New Normal
Page 140

CHAPTER 23
Into the Hills
Page 146

Author's Note
Page 150

Extra Bits!
Page 154

This book is dedicated to all the remarkable people who protect, preserve and restore our wild places. Thank you.

1
The Announcement

What on earth …
 She must be joking, right?
 I don't even know these people!

Picture the scene. Miss Cuthbertson wanders into the classroom as if Christmas had come early – *very* early, as it's only April. She looks around the room with her *'this is so exciting, isn't it'* face. My stomach sinks and my heart clenches in my chest. And then she lobs her missile.

'Ahem. Listen. As part of our transition to secondary school, we have come up with a really, REALLY exciting project. There will be an outdoor bound residential trip, just as we announced before. Haha – but there is a twist …' By now her smile is almost deranged. 'For your expedition, you will be teamed up with pupils from other schools!

How wonderful – it'll give you a chance to bond with young people from all around the city before you meet them at the Academy in August. Friendships *blah*, resilience *blah*, nature *blah* overcoming challenges together *blah blah* …'

I only take in small snippets of what follows. The Cuth drones on, but I don't think anyone is listening anymore. With a little relief, I notice that I'm not the only one looking around the room in distress – practically all the blood has drained from our collective faces. Even Sorley looks a little less big-headed than he normally does.

Come to think of it, if there happens to be a silver lining to this mother-of-all-calamitous-clouds, it's that I'll be able to avoid that boy for a few days.

But this is a dire disaster – there is no other expression for it. Or maybe there is. *Catastrophe? Utter ruin?*

'What are you talking about, Kenzie? Shut up!' a voice beside me hisses.

Oh no, I did it again. I said it aloud.

'You and your big words all the time. Think you're so clever, don't ya.'

I don't have a big-word-answer to that, so I don't bother. Claudia and her posse can think what they like.

Thankfully, the Cuth hasn't noticed. How could she, when she is in full flow about the transformative magic of mountain air, or whatever she is going on about now. '… and we will be announcing the groups after lunch,' she finishes.

A forest of hands shoots up as soon as she stops to breathe, but she waves us away impatiently, much like

9

Granny shoos away flies. 'No more time for questions now – the lunch bell is about to ring. And you'll find out soon enough. But do not worry. Most of you will have at least one person from our class in your expedition group, so there will be a familiar f—'

She is drowned out by the lunch bell. If she wanted to dismiss us table by table in an orderly manner, she can think again. We flee in a stampede of uproar past the unfortunate younger pupils who push themselves into the coat racks at the side of the corridor for safety. In the lunch hall, I wolf down my sandwich, shuddering whenever I hear the others mention mountains, expeditions or the names of the other schools. I don't join in. They wouldn't listen anyway.

The truth is, I find it hard enough to endure the people in my own class, never mind people I don't actually know. As for the thought of hiking up hills with complete strangers – well you might as well ask me to tap-dance across a tightrope.

Over Niagara Falls.

Let's be clear:

1. I don't do mountains.
2. I don't do strangers.
3. Let's face it, I barely do friends.

After lunch I find myself back in my seat without much of an idea of how I got there. I just want it to be over. The Cuth has other ideas, though, taking us out for a bracing jog three times around the school building. I can see right through her – she is not going to announce the groups until the very end of the school day so no one will have a chance to complain. Teachers will do anything for an easy life! With every step, I slam my trainers down hard on the ground at the injustice of it all. Running I can handle. Running is safe! Climbing mountains, I have a sneaking feeling, may be less so. Behind me most of the class puff loudly while Sorley is almost out of sight ahead of us all. Of course he is!

I must have set the world record for fastest PE changeover in my life as I sprint into the classroom and throw myself onto my seat. To be honest, I have no idea why I am so desperate to know. The names won't mean anything to me anyway.

'You're keen, Kenzie – no dithering today then,' my teacher jokes.

To say that I'm not up for banter is an understatement, so I don't laugh along. *Get on with it, Cuth.*

'Everyone here? Good, good. Ahem, listen now. Here.' She waits until all are seated and brandishes a densely printed sheet of blue paper. 'This is the letter to take home to your parents. It gives the details of transport arrangements, of the expedition schedule, details of the expedition leader and the names of others in your group. On the reverse you will find a kit list. Don't lose it. Tents will be provided by the outdoor centre on the day and their weight will be split between all participants. I'm sure you will all make the school very proud of your conduct, and we will see you bright and early on Monday.'

Her timing is better this time – the bell rings just as she

finishes her sentence, and she looks smug as a slug to have nailed it like that.

She fans the letters out on a table beside the door for us to pick up. I have to wait an agonising 30 seconds or so before it is my turn.

And then I wish I had never looked.

In fact, I wish I had never been born.

I don't do mountains.

Or strangers.

I barely do friends.

But I absolutely, categorically, emphatically do NOT do Sorley Mackay.

2
Hostile Habitats

I drift into the school library as the rest of my classmates are pouring out of the front door for the weekend.

That in itself is nothing new. As a library prefect, I often do a bit of tidying and sorting at lunchtimes or after school. Not today – today I know exactly what I'm looking for. The best way to be prepared is to be forearmed. *Where are the books about the Scottish hills?*

I slide my hand along the non-fiction section. Aha, a book of hill walks in the Scottish Highlands. A picture book on Scottish wildlife featuring a dancing capercaillie. A hefty volume called *Hostile Habitats* which just about puts the fear of death in me with its title, although it ends up being about geology and weather and wildlife and stuff. It's 'aimed at hillwalkers and climbers', it claims on

the first page. *Not* aimed at girls who love books but hate mountains and strangers and unexpected dangers. I sigh. Some of the pictures are mesmerising though, especially the sections on birds and animals. There is a running mountain hare – surprisingly grey – and a red squirrel jumping from branch to branch. I can't take my eyes off a kind of zebra version of a duck called the black-throated diver. Mostly though it's rocks, and landscapes with fog hanging low in the glens and blue skies above, sometimes with a lean-looking walker standing on a rocky outcrop gazing down at it all.

Oh man. That'll be me next, right?

I snort at the thought. Somehow that turns into a sob. Thank goodness I'm alone in here. *Get yourself together*, I tell myself. I water the plant at the centre of the room while I slowly count to ten. With shaky hands, I fill in the borrow slips for my pile of mountain books and place them in the librarian's box. Getting the books into my schoolbag turns into a bit of a wrestling match. Girl versus bag – but girl prevails. It was pretty full to start with, but now it's practically bursting. Oh well, I don't have all that far to walk.

I set off towards the front door. Normally I wouldn't mind school like this, all calm and quiet. Transformed, suddenly chilled-out teachers meander along the corridors balancing cups of tea and piles of photocopying, and the first cleaners come in, pulling blue tunics on over their trackies. Not another kid in sight. On any other day, this would relax me, but with every step my hefty bag serves as a reminder that I am heading to the mountains (argh!) with a bunch of strangers (aargh!) and Sorley Mackay (AAARGH!) which makes me want to wail and, let's be honest, faint.

Wait. *Faint ...*

That gives me an idea.

A very, very good idea.

Perhaps all is not lost!

Despite the weight pulling on my shoulders, I lengthen my strides along the road, and I feel almost okay by the time I run up the stairs towards our flat. Mum will be home already; she finishes early on Fridays.

I mentally rehearse my instructions to myself. *Timing will be everything, and I must keep it subtle. I will begin with coughing – they always do that in movies and next thing you know, they're dead. If I go off my food a little later, she'll have no choice but to let me miss the trip. Three days of books and telly and being pampered instead of the Sorley-scape of my nightmares.*

Great plan, Kenzie. Great, great plan. Genius, in fact.

I reach for the door handle and push.

What is that? I press harder. It takes all of my weight and that of my stuffed schoolbag to finally force the door of our flat open. Music blares out from the kitchen and Mum is singing along loudly before yelling, 'Is that you Mary?'

She is the only one in the world who calls me Mary – I often wonder what possessed her to call me that in the first place. I don't even know when it started, but 'Mary Mackenzie' became 'Kenzie' and I like to keep it that way. When I'm an adult I'll change my name on my passport too so that no one, NO ONE, can accidentally call me Mary.

'Hi Mum! Yes, I'm home.' I look around. 'Erm … Mum? What is all this?'

But even as the question comes out of my mouth, I realise – I know exactly what this is.

And worse, it messes with my great, genius plan.

3
More than a Match

Mum comes into view, beaming. Her red hair is tied back with a scarf, and beads of sweat glisten on her neck.

'Surprise, kiddo!'

I stare at the floor, strewn with plastic-wrapped items. Most unwelcome plastic-wrapped items.

Mum doesn't notice – or pretends not to. After all, I am her daughter, and she knows me well enough to read the signs.

She wipes her forehead. 'I've only just carried all this up from the car. Brilliant, isn't it? The email from the school about your mountain trip came through this morning, so I thought I'd print the kit list at work and see what I could get on the way back. The outdoor shop by the hospital had a sale. Look! Just *look* at all this!'

Her voice is doing backflips of excitement as she points out equipment, like a tour guide points out landmarks to impressed tourists. 'Rucksack, waterproof and all. Waterproof trousers. A rain jacket, also waterproof. A nice lightweight water bottle. And look at that, a sleeping bag – look how small it packs down! They say that tents will be provided, but here is a camping mattress for you to sleep on to keep you comfy. Thermal leggings in case it gets cold at night—'

'But Mum …' I try to look concerned for her, but she shakes her head.

'Don't worry about the money, kiddo – Granny wanted to help out, so it's all right. And you haven't seen the best thing yet. Look, look, look!' She twists around to present me with a rectangular box. I feel even worse knowing that my Granny paid for some of this – she lives in a tiny but dead expensive room in a care home and can't have much money to spare. Reluctantly, I accept the box and open the lid. 'Shoes?' I croak.

'Walking boots!' she exclaims triumphantly. 'What do you think of that, eh? Huh? Do you like them?'

Her eyes shine and however much I want to be truthful, I just can't. 'Yeah, nice,' I offer. 'Really cool.'

'Try them on!' she insists. 'The fleece too.'

Five minutes later, I stand in front of the mirror in Mum's bedroom and don't recognise myself. Thick-soled boots, walking socks, the vibrant red of a waterproof coat. Mum fiddles with the hood and adjusts the sleeves with their Velcro and somehow, I let it all happen.

'Perfect!' she breathes and stands back, fishing for something in her pocket. I grimace at my reflection before spotting the scissors.

'NO! Mum, wait, what are you doi—'

SNIP.

'Hang on, Mum, what if—'

SNIP SNIP SNIP.

'MUM!' I protest for the third time. 'You're cutting all the labels off.'

She doesn't respond to me stating the obvious. She continues wielding the scissors until the job is complete.

'I know!' she declares with a wink.

'But now we can't—'

'Return them to the shop?' she completes my sentence, grinning knowingly before continuing in a mock-sad voice. 'No, I suppose we can't.'

I groan in frustration.

'But it all fits, so I suppose that's all right,' she continues lightly. 'And you, Mary Mackenzie, can forget about pretending to be ill before the trip – just in case that option had crossed your mind. This expedition will be the making of you, and I am not letting you throw a chance like that away.'

My mouth falls open.

She just laughs and pulls me into a hug.

'Do better next time, kiddo. One step ahead of you as always, eh? Nice try. Better check the dinner.'

With her at work and me at school, the slow cooker works harder than either of us, ten hours a day. It smells good, I will say that. Half-heartedly, I resume flipping through the opening pages of *Hostile Habitats*.

'*For better or for worse, Scotland's mountain weather imposes itself on every day that we spend in the hills, and can range from glorious sunshine to life-threatening blizzards …*'

What?

LIFE-THREATENING?

I cast the heavy volume away (maybe to punish it for freaking me out) and turn my attention to a slimmer fact book about famous mountaineers instead. For a while, I read the tale of the two brave men who climbed Everest for the first time. I particularly like the name of one: Tenzing Norgay. Now that is a name worth having, rolling off the tongue like that – words are so cool! I say it several times over and lose myself in their adventure before remembering: this is not just a story about others.

Me, Kenzie, in the mountains. Let *that* sink in for a moment.

On second thoughts, DON'T. It's too scary.

It's ridiculous taking people like me into the hills. It's proper dangerous out there. Paths are steep. We could fall. We could break arms or legs. We could die.

After a stressful dinner during which I imagine what it may feel like to have a heart attack, I'm in bed, clutching my hot water bottle even though it's April. I won't be able to sleep in this state. *Enough panicking, Kenzie. ENOUGH! Use your brain*!

There will be a way out.

Oh. And I think I may have just thought of it.

Soundlessly, I slide my duvet off and tiptoe to the bedroom door. Squeezing through is not so very hard, nor is sneaking downstairs, taking great care to avoid the fifth step from the bottom which creaks. Mum's gentle snores on the sofa punctuate the muffled sounds of politicians debating something or other on the telly.

I feel like a spy on a mission.

Holding my breath, I unlock the porch door as quietly as possible. The cold night air creeps through my pyjamas and gnaws at my skin. Into the lane. My heart thunders in my chest.

'And once again, kiddo, you've got to do better than that.'

Sudden light streams from the porch with Mum's silhouette sharply outlined, her hands on her hips.

I hurriedly extract my arms and head fully from the recycling bin.

Mum's mouth is a tight line. 'Nice try, my girl. Newsflash: I know what you're like! And rest assured, your mother is more than a match for you. Those receipts and labels went into the stove as soon as you went to bed. There's nothing but ashes left. You're going, my girl, and that is that. Inside, now.'

I would love to have a comeback, but my brain is empty. I've got nothing. Brushing wastepaper shreds and pieces of plastic from the sleeves of my pyjamas, I have no choice but to join her at the table. Her normally smiling face has turned serious.

'All right, kiddo. Time for the talk.'

I roll my eyes.

'I know you feel nervous about the trip, but that is how we all build confidence. By doing things that are hard and coming out on the other side. By realising that we can *do hard things*, see what I mean?'

I am about to protest, but something stops me. Perhaps the way she pauses before *hard things*. *Hard things*, like parenting all on her own when she had counted on a fairytale marriage that would last for ever and ever.

But this isn't about Mum. This is about me.

'That's not fair, Mum. It's not that I don't try to do hard things. It's this particular trip. And it's about *who* I have to do the hard things *with!* There are two people in my group I don't even know. I don't even KNOW them! And …' I stop to swallow down my disgust before I can even get the words out. 'Then there is Sorley Mackay.'

Mum looks at me. Infuriatingly, the corners of her mouth twitch upwards, barely there, but I notice it. 'It's late. This conversation,' she announces, 'is over.'

And with that, she rises to switch off the lights. Defeated, I slouch back to my bed.

Maybe a heart attack wouldn't be so very bad.

It would get me out of this mess!

I finally fall into a fitful sleep, the towering shape of my new hillwalking equipment looming like a menacing shadow in the corner of the room.

4
Departure

Why is it that days stretch like old chewing gum when you want them to pass quickly? Why is it that minutes, hours, mornings and nights fly by when all you need is time to think of an escape?

The day of the trip arrives, uninvited like a wasps' nest. And, although I hate to admit it, my chances of outwitting my insistent mother are diminishing towards zero. Whatever my latest scheme, she is onto me. When I complain of stomach-ache the day before leaving, she bundles me out of the door to my piano lesson. When I suggest I may have a fever the night before, she mercilessly measures my temperature and declares me a perfectly healthy specimen. I am running out of options. Around midnight, I reluctantly face the inevitable. I am going.

The bursting backpack is waiting for me by the door. The waterproof jacket and trousers hang over the chair. The clock tick-tick-ticks towards seven o'clock when the alarm will ring for my doom.

Now, my best hope is to get some sleep and, hopefully, survive. And for this, I have a simple strategy: ignore everyone.

Breathing deeply, I repeat this new mantra.

Ignore everyone. Ignore everyone. Ignore everyone.

This I can do. In fact, I believe it to be my superpower.

As soon as the alarm rings, I am half-girl, half-robot. The real Kenzie has retreated to a tiny part of my brain, and the rest of my body gets ready automatically, giving my mother nothing but half-answers and shrugs.

Somehow, I find myself at the door, dressed top to toe in clothing that is just wrong for me. Mum compensates with extra energy and extra cheerfulness – all the things old people are not supposed to have but that my mother exudes in abundance. Yes, I am still me – Kenzie who reads books and knows words other people don't. And I know that thirty-eight isn't that old, but I am in the mood to be mean today.

'Hurry kiddo! We can't miss that bus!'

We *could*, and that wouldn't be the end of the world, but she won't want to hear that.

The truth is that, deep down, I can't bear to get on the wrong side of Mum. I can't disappoint her, I just can't. She's all I've got. But it's worse than that: I'm all *she's* got, too. I can't let her down like Dad did.

The intermittent raindrops make a funny noise on the waterproof hood. I've never had a jacket like this before, and strangely, I don't hate the sound. It's the sound of adventure. Then I remember: adventures are good things for people in books. But I am not a person in a book. I am Kenzie. I like to *read* about adventures, not actually have them.

But what I do and don't like seems to be of little importance right now. Mum runs alongside me, carrying the enormous backpack. Far too soon, the school comes into view. Claudia's posse have gathered by the car park. A little way along, Sorley and the football gang shuffle towards a bright orange bus, and his voice is the only one I can hear, bragging about mountains he has climbed and how fit he is. I place myself in the middle of the two groups. The only good thing is the way Miss Cuthbertson shuts Sorley up when she takes the register. In front of all these parents, he has no choice but to be quiet.

Our teacher begins: 'Right, morning everyone. Ahem, as you know, all the participating schools will drop their pupils off at a car park. Most of the expeditions will set out from there. Each group has a different route, so you will not encounter others. Pupils will also have an experienced mountain guide with them at all times. He or she will keep you safe and offer practical support.' She lowers her reading glasses and peers over them with raised eyebrows. 'But make no mistake – this expedition's aim is threefold. You will grow more independent. You will grow more resilient. And you will forge connections with new friends.' She holds our gaze, as if daring us to laugh. No one does. Until Sorley raises his voice. 'Yes, quite! Well said, Miss! Exactly my sentiment, and I feel sure that I speak for all of us.'

Ninety-nine percent of us know he is being sarcastic, especially when he places his hand over his heart and closes his eyes in a fake moment of reflection. For some reason, Miss Cuthbertson isn't sure enough to give him a row, despite most of us stifling giggles. She decides to move on as swiftly as possible. 'Now, no time for dithering. Say your goodbyes and get on that bus!'

How does he do it? How does he slither out of trouble like a greased piglet, every single time?

I will have ages to contemplate this on the trip. My enormous backpack keeps me company as others in front and behind me chat excitedly about what lies ahead. Their words blur into a mishmash of sounds. Needless to say, Sorley's booming voice carries above the din. I wish it didn't. *Goodness, I can't endure this for three days. I just can't.*

On the other side of the windowpane, the landscape changes from a built up town to suburbs and endless estates of identical houses, to interspersed clusters of buildings. The road gets windier, first hugging the shore of a loch, then crossing a churning river, then heading up through thinning woods. At the very back of the bus, someone retches. Could it be Sorley?

No, I am not that lucky. It is Claudia who insists on wearing full makeup for reasons best known to herself. I feel almost sorry for her, her eyeliner stark against her green-tinged skin. She has plenty of girls fussing over her, so I turn back to face forwards. The clouds have parted, and a single shaft of sunlight illuminates the road in front of us and crowns the mountain tops with bright gold. It looks like an illustration from a fairy tale book. Just as I think about that, we are thrown to the right as the bus makes a sharp turn. Poor Claudia heaves again. The engine stops. And then all of us fall silent.

I mean, really silent.

The place that passes for a car park is muddy and strewn with sticks and bracken. Whichever way I turn, I can't see a single house anymore. Not one.

I think we all feel it – whatever *this* is, it's bigger than us, and we feel small, insignificant, vulnerable. We shuffle and scuffle out of the bus where the breeze carries a damp drizzle. Uncertainly, I drop my bag and fumble for the sheet of paper with our group names. I can sense Sorley's eyes drilling into the back of my head, and I suspect he is not thrilled with the combination either, but neither of us can help it now.

Let it be over soon. Let it be over and done with and let everything be as it was before. It's a prayer of sorts. Gradually, the chatter around me resumes. Once I have looked at the landscape (and there is a lot of it), I decide to observe Miss Cuthbertson who tucks her greying curls back into her bun and narrows her eyes to be able to read her watch. She frowns at the bus driver. Something wordless passes between them. Tension? Disappointment?

Whatever it was, it is replaced with relief at the sound of a faraway engine noise.

All of us crane our necks as two more buses squelch into the car park, followed finally by the rat-tat-tat of a minibus which has seen better days. The lower half of the vehicle is so mud-splattered that it's hard to tell what colour is hiding beneath it, but the top half is another matter – spray-painted, graffiti-style, and not at all artistically. I imagine the fit my mother would have if I took a can of spray-paint to our little car.

'Ah, good. That's everyone here now,' Miss Cuthbertson announces to no one in particular. She strides towards the adults emerging from the minibus. 'Hello, it's good to meet you. You must be the instructors.'

By now, the place is filled with people and bags and the buses begin to pull away. There is half-hearted hand-shaking and embarrassed laughing and some awkward standing around, and that's just the adults.

The busload of pupils from our school eye up the busloads of kids we don't know.

They ogle back at us. The last of the chatter dies away. No one moves.

5
Into the Wild

Finally, the adults take the initiative. I think part of my brain shuts down for a moment – I only half register the shuffling and name calls and pushing and dragging of bags. All I know is that everything around me is chaos and I do not like it. I do not like the Cuth's shrieks, and her forced laughter. I do not like the fact that the person now shoved to my side is Sorley Mackay. I do not like the close proximity of the other two pupils I find myself standing nose to nose with. And now a tall, sinewy man with greying hair and wind-whipped skin tries to usher us four away from the others, like a predator would isolate vulnerable prey. If this was a wildlife programme, the voiceover would say something about the skill of the hunter and the impending doom of the duped young.

Wait. Someone just said my name. Maybe. The tall man – our instructor. He is looking at me intently. Is he waiting for an answer?

'Mary, yeah?' he says, probably the second time around.

'Kenzie,' I correct him, but my mind is swimming again. All the pandemonium is too much, and I feel like scrunching up my eyes – as if that was going to solve anything at all. I hear Claudia snigger somewhere behind me.

The man consults a clipboard. 'Fine, Kenzie it is. I don't like my first name either. Right guys, I'm Ivor Baird, but everyone calls me Bairdy. I'm your mountain guide for this trip. Our group is actually setting off a good few miles south of here. No faffing about in the foothills – we're doing the real mountains, us! So, Sorley, Rupert, Mariam, and Ma … I mean, Kenzie – yes, that's it, all here. We're good. Over there.' He points to the mud-splattered vehicle behind the buses.

I am thinking that 'good' is not quite the right word when the skinny boy Rupert interrupts, floppy fringe blowing in the wind. 'How long have you done mountain guiding, Bairdy?'

Oh, to be able to make conversation as easily as that! How can Rupert be so confident?

I fall in behind them, followed by the Cuth, to my dismay. She all but shoves us onto the muddy minibus, slams the door and pats it for good measure. Probably to make sure we cannot escape. Bairdy gets behind the wheel and revs up the engine. 'Right, gang, another twenty minutes or so into the glen. Adventure begins here.'

I feel sick. Teachers and fellow pupils shrink into the distance as we turn and speed away. First of all, the road makes all other windy and twisty roads seem wimpy. Secondly, I am on a minibus driven by a complete stranger. Thirdly, I have only Sorley for company. I don't know the others, so they don't count. Soon our route is more pothole than road surface. Eventually, Bairdy pulls off the dirt track altogether.

'Is this a car park?' Sorley wants to know.

'The nearest we are going to get to one,' grins our guide. He jumps out of the vehicle, making a huge splash in a muddy puddle on the ground. We hesitate. 'Come on then, guys,' he laughs. 'If a little water puts you off, it's a bad start. Who wants the map? I'll do the navigating, obviously, but I thought you might like an idea, so I picked one up at the tourist office.'

Rupert raises his hand and becomes the proud recipient of a leaflet. With a grin, Bairdy pushes the door, which is basically the whole side of the bus, closed. 'Great, team. Okay, get your packs on your backs and let's go.' He distributes the boys' and girls' tents between the four of us. I get the poles, which is not too bad in the grand scheme of things.

I cast about for a café, or a toilet, or a path, or a road sign, or anything else to pin my vanishing hopes to. Nope. Nothing.

All right! Survival mode. I swing the backpack onto my shoulders, hoping to portray an air of confidence. We all know that predators smell fear. I am surrounded by four of them, and I must not let them see me panic. Subconsciously, I chant under my breath. *Ignore everyone. Ignore everyone. Breathe, and breathe, and breathe …*

At least I can get a good look at the guide now that he stops to adjust the straps on his own pack. I mostly glanced away when he was looking at me. He is tall and skinny with broad shoulders, but his arm muscles tighten and ripple as he lifts the weight of his enormous pack, with seemingly little effort. His boots are dirty and the laces threadbare, his trousers loose. He doesn't wear a jacket like we do, although a waterproof garment is poking out from the top of his pack. Instead, he dons some sort of waistcoat with more pockets than I thought were possible to fit onto a single item of clothing. Lively blue eyes crinkle beneath bushy eyebrows in his weatherbeaten face. One corner of his mouth curls up in a smirk. Then his eyes come to rest on me again, and I quickly look away.

'All good. Ready,' he mumbles, mostly to himself. He turns off the path and squelches into the mud towards the gathering clouds. The boys lope after him, trying to outdo each other by keeping up as casually as possible. As it dawns on me how stupid they are being, I realise: if I don't hurry up, I am going to be left behind before the expedition has even started.

I'd almost forgotten about the girl called Mariam. Now she walks beside me, her thick black plait swinging left and right. She mostly looks ahead, although from time to time, I feel her peek aside and up at me. Up because I am the best part of a head taller than her. I try not to reciprocate.

But I can feel it – she is uncertain of this whole thing too.

'Wait!' Bairdy has only walked a little distance from the vehicle when he stops himself. 'Man, gang, you're messing with my head! What a disaster.'

Despite his heavy pack, he jogs back towards the minibus, sending high splashes of dark-brown water onto his trousers. He opens the back doors and then it happens: a streak of gold bounds out, launches itself into the first puddle, yelps with joy, wags its tail faster than the grass can blow in the wind and zigzags around out of control. The dog doesn't stay still long enough for me to get a proper look at it, but I reckon there is a bit of collie and a bit of retriever in the mix, and whatever else. Bairdy locks up the vehicle again and joins me and Mariam.

'Can't believe I nearly forgot him! Gotta bring Drookit, don't I?'

Once my eyes have locked onto their target, I can confirm that the dog looks cute, so I wait a moment until it comes near, expecting it to run past me and ahead with the boys. But oh no.

The massive, shaggy fur-missile hits me head-on. I never had a hope of staying on my feet after that, but for a second or two, a kind of slow motion plays out. A flash of concern crosses Bairdy's face. Mariam throws out her arm to steady me. I flail, reach for her hand, and miss. There is a roar of wind, but perhaps the sound is in my own ears. My backpack conspires with gravity and despite my contortions, I land backwards in the marshy mud. Now it's my turn to be splattered with unspeakable stuff.

'Get up quick,' urges Bairdy, laughing hard, grabbing my sodden pack and pulling me by its handle. 'If you just lie there, you'll be soaked through to the skin.'

Behind him, I barely register Sorley Mackay giggling and, infuriatingly, pulling a disposable camera from his jacket pocket. I clamber to my feet, dripping. 'It was your dog that did it!' I mutter, tears welling up in my eyes. 'Why didn't you tell us that you had a dog with you? Is that even allowed?'

Looking across at Mariam, I can tell she is asking herself the same questions. On second glance, she has changed completely. Her whole body is tense and the colour has drained from her face. Her eyes do not leave the dog which is rolling itself in heather and weeds.

Bairdy shrugs. 'Okay, I'll come clean! I'm not *supposed* to take him on expeditions, but I get paid for these trips, and I can't very well leave him, can I? He does no harm; he's dead friendly. You're gonna love him! I call him Drookit because he just loves the water, he does.'

'I'm not great with dogs.' It is barely there, the voice. The first time I've heard Mariam speak.

But Bairdy hasn't heard, I think. 'Okay, reboot! Let's go, gang! I've delayed us enough, and the mountains are calling. Come on Drookit! Let's go camping in the hills with our new friends!'

The trousers stick to my backside and the wet fabric rubs against my legs, but I have no choice but to break into a trot to catch up with our guide and the boys. Behind me, Mariam follows warily. Thankfully, Drookit ignores her, but he seems to have marked me out for special attention. First, he circles me. Then he prances beside me. By the time we take our first rest by a tinkling stream, he rests his head on my lap and looks up with a face that would melt anyone's heart. It's like he is apologising.

When the boys throw sticks for him and Drookit takes no notice of them and licks my hand instead, I smile for the first time in a week.

It isn't until mid-afternoon that we see another human being in the distance, cresting the mountain opposite us for a moment before dropping back out of view.

Bairdy's hands shoot to his binoculars, and he hurriedly lifts them to his eyes. He mumbles angrily, though I can't make out the words.

'What's up, Big Man?' Sorley wants to know in his infuriating, irritating, inappropriate, overfamiliar way.

'Nothing,' our leader grunts. But his features have darkened.

6
Opinions

It takes half an hour of Drookit lolloping around his master's feet for Bairdy's mood to lift again. But then I almost wished it hadn't.

I have never met anyone with so many opinions. I never thought I'd meet anyone who would express them so freely.

It begins innocently enough. Bairdy points out the wildflowers in the bogs and on rocks along the path: mountain thyme with its tiny pink flowers, endless spreads of bog-cotton, and blaeberry blossoms which, he says, will turn into edible berries by late summer (I am not eating that sort of thing!). Once you look closely, there are tiny yellow flowers everywhere – although I missed what Bairdy called them. Each flower is made up of four identical heart-shaped petals, and according to Bairdy, they were used for treating tummy upsets.

At least we are not racing forward anymore, so Mariam and I can easily keep up. Bairdy's pace has slowed to an amble, if that.

'Shouldn't we be moving on?' Sorley asks. I half-heartedly agree. The sooner we get there the sooner it will be over, I think – knowing better than to say that bit aloud.

Our leader laughs. 'What's your hurry, Sorley? It's not a race, my friend! Now, look at the hillside. What do you see?' We remain quiet. Bairdy tries again: 'All right. What don't you see up there?'

'Trees,' Mariam volunteers shyly.

'Exactly. We have a million deer in Scotland. Any young native trees don't stand a chance to grow beyond small saplings. If you do see trees, they are likely to be plantations, monocultures of the same types, instead of the diverse native species we *should* see here. And look to the skies – where are the raptors?'

'Birds of prey,' I comment when Mariam's and Sorley's faces look blank. *Don't these people read?*

Bairdy nods. 'Yes – there should be hundreds – and not so very long ago, there were. You can read about it in the diaries of gamekeepers, even a couple of hundred years back. And before that, there were wolves too!'

I gulp at the thought of packs of wolves howling in these hills. *But really, who reads centuries-old gamekeepers' diaries? This man is mad.*

Bairdy's face relaxes into a determined grin. 'All we

need is the will to restore it all, and nature will do the rest. And to answer your question, Sorley, I will take my time if that's all right with you. It's all about the experience, isn't it? You had a wee camera with you there, didn't you? Take some snaps. Notice things! Learn to appreciate the hills. Enjoy them.'

Enjoy them? I make an involuntary sound of disgust and quickly turn to see if anyone has heard. *Oh no, Mariam was right behind me.* To my surprise, she doesn't look as if she is about to make fun of me. Actually, in her face I see some of the pain I feel myself. I give her an uncertain smile and to my astonishment, she returns it. She takes a couple of faster steps to catch up with me.

'Kenzie, I am terrified of that dog,' she admits, her voice shaky. I follow her pointing finger to see Sorley and Rupert wrestling Drookit on the ground. Bits of heather and goodness-knows-what stick out of Sorley's hair. Rupert's branded clothing seems to withstand the mud better than Sorley's. I feel the wind blow my own clothing dry, bit by bit.

'Well, I'm not about to do what the boys are doing and get myself soaked again, let's be honest. But Mariam, that dog is harmless, honestly. It's cute, actually.'

She doesn't look so sure. Without a word, she rolls up her right sleeve to reveal a patchwork of scars on her forearm. I look from her face to the arm and then to Drookit. It takes my brain a few seconds to process what I am seeing. 'Wait – a dog did that to you?'

Without a further word, she nods, rolls her sleeve down

again and drops to the very back of our group, placing me firmly between herself and Drookit, like a Kenzie-shaped shield.

It must be hard for her. Suddenly I feel a powerful wave of anger and resentment for the boys who are chasing each other to loud barks from the dog. I turn to Bairdy. 'Aren't you going to tell them off? For winding your dog up like this?'

As soon as my demand is out of my mouth, I regret saying anything at all. He narrows his eyes before answering, extra-calmly, and enunciating every syllable: 'No, Kenzie, I have no plans to tell them off. Do *you* think they shouldn't be allowed to have fun?'

I can't very well tell him that this is exactly what I think. Instead, I drop back, hovering around Mariam but unsure what to say to her.

Consequently, I say nothing.

Bairdy resumes his tour-guide style monologue of opinions. There is no end to what the man has a problem with. He doesn't think it's fair that a few rich people own most of Scotland's wild places. He wishes that there were more trees. Apparently, there was something called 'The Great Caledonian Forest' or something, but now all the hills are covered with heather and low shrubs, and he tells us that this is to make grouse and deer thrive, which rich people then shoot. I get a bit confused about that – what's the point in creating ideal conditions for a creature you are then going to kill? I must ask him to explain that sometime.

Sorley and Rupert really get interested when Bairdy mentions there would be wolves and lynx in these hills again if he had his way, especially lynx. Sorley howls in a fake way and Rupert joins in, and it annoys me more than I can say that Sorley seems to have made a friend so easily and I have not. Worse, our guide seems to laugh at every joke and quip the boys make.

'Ah, okay, and now look! Look at that! That's what I mean, kids.' Bairdy points at a hillside some way into the distance. We stop and shade our eyes against the glare, but I can't see what he is on about.

'Looks like any other hillside to me,' I offer eventually. I am not good with awkward silences.

'That's exactly what I'm getting at,' our leader explains. 'They're all the same, and they shouldn't be. And see those black patches among the brown and green? That's evidence of heath burning, or muirburn.'

Rupert chips in: 'Is that when they burn the plants deliberately? It encourages growth, right?'

Bairdy shakes his head. 'It encourages only *new growth*. Ideal conditions for animals you can shoot, like grouse. Think how wonderfully diverse everything would be if we allowed nature to take its course. Think of it! Trees, the lungs of the planet, right here. This place should be like a mosaic, not a patchwork with straight lines. We should be seeing Scots pine, juniper, birch, willow, rowan, aspen and more, and lichens and mosses, too. If we had this, we'd get a bit of biodiversity back.'

He has trailed off, lost in his own vision of beavers and

lynx and wolves and trees and goodness knows what else. I look around. I'm pretty sure there would be fewer walkers like Bairdy out here if you had a good chance of being chased by a pack of wolves.

We have all lost the determined strides of the early morning. The path has become steeper, and I feel the straps of my backpack cut into my shoulders with every step as we reach the tree line. A seemingly endless expanse of heather opens up, reminding me of a book I once read about the arctic tundra. Even Drookit stays closer to his master now, although he pops back from time to time to get a stroke from me. He likes it behind his ears most. Every time the dog rubs against my legs, Mariam emits a sort of whimpering sound. I don't think she can help it.

'How much longer, Big Man?' Sorley asks, and for once I'm grateful. I'm sure we all want to know the answer to that.

'Just up there – there is a nice dry-ish flat bit of ground where we can set up camp. Views are great there, especially in the morning. That direction there is east, so the sun rises over there.' He points.

There is nothing for it, we summon all our remaining strength for the climb. At times I even have to use my hands to steady myself on the steep slope, but eventually we reach a dry and level patch among the heather and rocks.

'Great work, guys! Now – ever heard of a shieling?' Bairdy asks. 'It may not seem likely to you, but people used to actually live in these mountains. During the grazing season, they took their cattle all the way up here. Look over there – see the pile of rocks? Most likely that was a hut. Shelter for whoever looked after the animals during the summer. Of course, the Clearances stopped all of that.'

We learned about the Highland Clearances in class last year when I still had Miss Forshaw, not the Cuth. I could never live in a place like this. It's hard to imagine that anyone ever did. Now there is animal poo everywhere, and plenty of tracks too. Rupert is about to get on his knees to dissect an owl pellet he has spotted with a couple of twigs when Bairdy interrupts. 'Time for that later. Let's set up camp first and get ourselves comfortable before it gets dark. Tents, everyone. Go, go, go!'

7
A Home in the Hills

'It goes over here! Slide it into that bit!'

I am not sure how Sorley got to oversee this whole operation, but somehow, he is bossing us around, erecting the first of two tents, while Bairdy has taken himself off to some large rocks a little distance away. Every few minutes, our instructor raises his binoculars to his eyes and takes some notes in a little leather notebook. Then he tucks it into one of his many pockets. I only notice this because I turn to watch him again and again, with growing resentment. *He* should be running this show, not flipping Sorley Mackay!

Rupert seems to have a more natural knack for logic and the boys' tent stands swiftly, with the four of us pulling and pegging it into place. Somehow, the poles of Mariam's and my tent do not want to stay bent in the right way, and the boys have much less interest in helping *us* than setting up their own shelter like a palace inside.

Again, I glance across to our leader. He's looking at the same ledge where we saw the figure earlier, I'm sure of it. *How can I get him to help us, without sounding like a crabby, cranky, cantankerous whiner?* I try to think of a humorous comment, but none comes. Plus, he doesn't seem in the mood for laughing – his eyebrows are all knotted again, and he mumbles under his breath. Something is definitely going on. Mariam keeps checking over her shoulder for Drookit, but he's lying at his master's feet, licking his paws.

My resolve crumbles. I'm about to break my number one survival strategy. The *ignore everyone* rule.

'Honestly, Mariam, that dog will not hurt you, you can relax. And I'm going to admit it, I'm a bit incompetent with stuff like this.' I gesture at the disarray of tentpoles, pegs and guy ropes at our feet.

Despite the tension in her face, she giggles. 'What, "incompetent"? Who even says words like that?'

'Me, apparently.'

She chuckles again. 'Yes you, "apparently"! There's another one! What's with the big words?'

I shrug, but I can't help smiling back. 'I like using them. All right, Mariam, I'm going to make this simple for you then: any idea where this bit goes?'

I hold up the shortest of the tent poles.

To my surprise she doesn't seem freaked out by that question. 'I think it goes … in the doorway, like this. Bends

round like that, and then we peg it into place here ... and here.'

Her voice is so quiet that I can barely hear it, but she is right – the whole thing looks like the diagram on the label now.

'Good,' she continues. 'And now we put the flysheet over the top like this, I think. We need to peg it tight – if it's too slack, the tent may leak.'

My mouth has fallen open. I look around, but no, nobody else has witnessed Mariam's moment of sheer brilliance, or heard a word of what she just said. Only me.

'Well done, Mariam. I think you're right! We've got it now.' My awe is completely genuine – I am truly impressed. We spend the next few minutes tightening guy ropes and pegging the last fluttering ends into place.

'Perfect,' I admire grudgingly, half relieved and half annoyed, with another resentful side glance at Bairdy. A sort of home in the hills. I will hate camping, no doubt. But the truth is, we managed to set up a tent in the middle of nowhere all on our own, without the help of our useless instructor.

He has wandered off a little way, binoculars perpetually to his eyes now. Giggles come from the boys' tent, and Mariam and I roll out our sleeping bags inside ours. 'Not too bad,' I mumble – more to myself than anyone else.

'Not too bad at all,' Mariam replies shyly and holds her hand up. Never in my life have high-fived anyone other than Mum. I am astonished at how good it feels.

Like a caveman, Bairdy finally decides to get involved

at the cooking stage. I had expected him to rub sticks together really fast like they do in the survival videos on YouTube.

'Are we making a campfire now?' Sorley demands. Perhaps he expected twigs too.

Bairdy laughs and shakes his head. 'No chance! It's far too dangerous to start fires in the mountains. Even the smallest spark can cause a wildfire, and once a wildfire starts it's really hard to stop. No, no – we'll do it properly and stick to one of these!' He produces a camping stove and a frying pan from the side pocket of his bag. Best of all, his bottomless bag contains an eight-pack of rolls and a packet of bacon, as well as a vegetarian version for Mariam who doesn't eat pork. Before long, the scent of freshly cooked bacon mingles with the mountain breeze. Nothing, NOTHING has ever smelled so good! One roll is more than enough for me, but Sorley and Rupert both have two each. Gluttons! I don't say that aloud though, because they will only ridicule me. I do, however, catch Mariam's eye across the glow of the stove. She casts a sideways glance at Drookit, sprawled out on his back at his master's feet, and grimaces at me. A grimace. A secret exchange just between the two of us. It's a new experience for me, and I find that I don't mind it at all. I may consider making an exception to my *ignore everyone* rule for Mariam. She seems all right.

As the western sky comes alive with fiery colour, our leader pours hot chocolate into our camping cups and finishes with a sprinkling of tiny marshmallows. I breathe deeply. People have hot chocolate in books all the time. I can't bring myself to admit this to the others, but never once have I had hot chocolate outside before. Rupert, on the other hand, looks like he has never done anything else in his life. I steal a sly peek at him while no one else is looking. He appears to have walked straight out of the Go Wild Store catalogue Mum left on the kitchen table in the vain hope that it would get me excited about the trip. There he sits with his wind-tousled hair and the floppy fringe I noticed before, all ruddy cheeks, waterproofs, walking boots – and that rapturous faraway expression on his face that says *I am one with the wilderness*. Sorley has kicked his boots off, and the fleeting thought crosses my mind that maybe I do not hate this quiet Sorley quite as much as I hate the everyday Sorley. Mariam moves around, shifting to whichever side of me does not have the dog on it.

And Bairdy? He rubs his hands together with glee.

8
Am Fear Liath Mòr

'Now, young mountaineers, hot chocolate calls for stories, and stories call for proper attention. Look around you! See those peaks? That's the way of the Lairig Ghru – the Gloomy Pass which cuts right through the Cairngorm mountains. It's a world of desolate heights up there: Cairn Toul, Braeriach, Ben MacDui and Cairn Gorm, as well as The Devil's Point.' I see Mariam shudder, but Bairdy continues, dropping his voice to barely above a whisper. 'The old Gaelic stories tell us that the *Sìdh* dwell up there.'

He pronounces it *shee* and I find myself mouthing the word after him under my breath.

'It means the "good people", but they are unpredictable and sometimes dangerous – that is the real reason why folk call them "good". Best not to upset the *Sìdh*, see? *Sìdh* can take on the forms of all sorts of creatures; they are shapeshifters.'

'Like what creatures?' The question is out of my mouth before I even realise.

Bairdy raises his eyebrows. 'As I said, all sorts. The giantess *Maggy Moulach* who appears waving her long hairy arms as a warning that danger is near. The *Cù-Sìth*, a spectral hound haunting the hills. Or the *Cat Sìth*, a black cat the size of a dog with a white spot on its chest and eyes that glow in the dark, a stealer of souls.'

I shiver. Drookit does not love the idea of dog-sized cats either. He creeps up beside me and starts licking my hand.

'But the creature I am going to tell you about right now is my favourite! Have any of you heard the story of *Am Fear Liath Mòr*?'

We exchange glances. Rupert looks like he may be about to say something, but he doesn't quite trust himself and closes his mouth again.

Bairdy's eyes glint with mischief. All around us, tendrils of mist form near the ground while above us the sky fades from yellow to orange, pink, and purple, eventually darkening to black.

He grins. 'Well, listen up then. *Am Fear Liath Mòr* is Gaelic for the Big Grey Man, said to haunt the summit of Ben MacDui.' Bairdy's voice has dropped to a melodious sing-song and even Sorley can't bring himself to interrupt. 'Few have caught a glimpse of him. A hulking body, seemingly made of the rocks themselves. Shoulders wider than a golden eagle's wingspan. Tall and tough as a tree.

Hidden in mountain mist, up there on the heights.'

Bairdy's eyes flit sideways and up – and ours follow, glancing up at the mountain crests around us, and the clouds above.

'The legend is as old as the hills,' our guide continues. 'The Grey Man is a creature of darkness. Most climbers hear him rather than see him – they hear his crunching, heavy steps on the gravel, and other strange noises until dread begins to paralyse their minds. But a few witnesses have reported seeing a tall, stony, dark-haired figure in the moonlight, walking slowly, always following, never resting.'

A tiny squeak leaves Mariam's mouth and the boys giggle mercilessly, but Bairdy hasn't heard, or he pretends he hasn't.

'*Am Fear Liath Mòr*'s presence is felt rather than proven, but on one occasion he is said to have charged at a mountaineer who fled as fast as he could down the mountain. The climber's friends ridiculed him, but he pointed out the giant footsteps the next morning. Coincidence? I really don't think so.'

Bairdy pauses dramatically, raising his eyes to the sky. 'Oh no!' His eyes widen and his body stiffens. 'Do you hear that?'

Drookit begins to growl. We glance about. Most of the colour has left Rupert's face. I feel it too – an oppressive, heavy silence which makes me shiver.

'HAHA! Got you!' Bairdy laughs suddenly, as Drookit howls with joy and wags his tail again. 'I trained the dog to growl on my signal, didn't I? Works a treat, every time! Your faces!' He chuckles so hard that we can't help laughing along out of sheer embarrassment.

'Right, enough for tonight. Drink up, guys.'

We down the last of our hot chocolate.

'Time to tuck yourselves in. Boys, if nature calls, head behind that rock to the left, and girls, the old shieling ruin for you. Means we're not going to have any unfortunate encounters overnight. Everyone got their torches?'

We mumble affirmatively.

Bairdy's tiny one-man tent, still in its bag, lies a little way off from ours. On the label it looks like the sort of thing a caterpillar may shed, barely fitting around a person. He must have seen me look. 'I'll set mine up in a bit, don't worry. It just pops up into shape and you peg it down. Takes seconds.'

'Are you not going to sleep too?' Sorley, and only Sorley, would be forward enough to ask the adult in charge that question.

Bairdy doesn't seem to mind. 'Not yet – gotta give Drookit the chance to do his dog stuff last thing, don't I. But then I'll turn in, too. A wee wander finishes the day off nicely.' His eyes flit to the ridge. He seems restless, as if he is not yet done for the night.

'Is that steep bit where we are going tomorrow, Bairdy?' Sorley sounds a tiny bit nervous if I am not much mistaken. But then this is Sorley, so I must have imagined that.

'Yes – my colleague will collect the minibus from where we left, and the day after tomorrow she'll pick us up in the village on the other side of that peak over there.'

He points well beyond the ridge to a summit piercing the lowering clouds. 'Weather is going to be more of a challenge tomorrow night, but we'll manage. Now, see you guys tomorrow. Don't do anything stupid like wandering off in the middle of the night.'

He laughs, but there is an edge to it.
Wander off in the night?
Is that guy for real?
No one would do that.
No one.

9
The Morning After

There is a good reason people don't share cramped spaces. How anyone sleeps in a tent like this is beyond me. I look at my watch at 21.36, startled by the high singing buzz of a bug in the tent. Mariam and I spend a less-than-enjoyable half-hour chasing it before claiming victory at 22.03. More watch checks at 23.57, at 01.45, and at 3.00 on the dot when I decide that, annoyingly, I need a wee. It takes all my concentration to wriggle the tent flap open, and for a moment, I am awestruck. Never in my whole life have I seen skies so dark and stars so bright, with a cloudy length of light that can only be the Milky Way. Once I'm done and have wiped my hands clean, it seems almost a shame to close the tent door again. Another hour later, I have reached a state somewhere between exhaustion and sleep and am convinced that I hear a scream in the wind.

'Kenzie … Did you hear that? Ugh, is it the Grey Man?' whispers Mariam, who is obviously awake too.

'Don't be scared, little one,' I reply mockingly, elbowing her to show her that I'm half-joking. Hopefully she'll understand that and won't take offence.

After that, sleep must have claimed me for its own, because the very next thing I remember is the walls of the tent caving in. Literally, really, and above all, noisily.

'Aaargh!'

'AAArghhh!' Mariam's cry is louder, shriller and a whole lot more heartfelt than mine because the caving walls of the tent are accompanied by loud barking – and I mean LOUD! Heavy outlines of Drookit's paws pummel our tent from the outside.

My head slowly assembles the pieces. We are in the middle of nowhere, shuddering in the misty light of early morning. And there is nothing but a flimsy tent wall between us and an agitated dog's teeth. I rub my forehead and the tent stops shaking for a moment – Drookit must be circling us. If only the barking would stop. If only Bairdy would call him away. Why doesn't he stop him?

I hear startled voices from the boys' tent too.

'What time is it?' Mariam leans in close to me, her hands over her ears, and I check my watch.

'Just before seven,' I shout through the barking.

'What?'

'Just BEFORE SEVEN,' I yell louder to make myself heard over the din. The tent walls are caving in again, and once more I can see the clear outline of Drookit's front paws. 'He is going to ruin the tent like this.'

'I can't go out there,' Mariam hisses, every syllable laced with fear.

'Fine, I'll do it.' I can hardly hear myself think amid the barks, growls and whines, all blending into one another, but I bend my clammy body to wriggle out of my sleeping bag and attempt to undo the tent door with stiff fingers. Drookit seems to sense that someone is coming and redoubles his efforts, barking ever more frantically. Bairdy must be having a sleep as deep as the Mariana Trench. How anyone can stay down in this racket is beyond me.

And as it turns out, I am developing some of those opinions myself. When your fingers are cold and damp, the hardest thing to do is manoeuvre a zip. And what is everything in a camping context fastened with? This whole outdoor thing is stupid. Sleeping bag, zip. My fleece, zip. My trousers, zip. The tent flap, zip and zip again. I rest my case.

When I finally manage to wrestle through the tent flap and crawl out onto the dew-sodden grass, a muddy, soggy and smelly dog-missile launches itself at me once more and nearly knocks me back into the tent.

'Keep him out!' shrieks Mariam.

I quickly secure the tent flap again and rise and stretch. The boys' tent is still fully closed – they must be trying to go back to sleep. 'Drookit, boy, calm down. Drookit, shush!'

His high whines alternate with jumps, as he circles

himself in his excitement. Hard as I try, he will not settle or shut up.

'Drookit! That's enough! SIT!'

Eventually he obeys, but it takes me ages to calm the beast down enough to get a proper look at him.

At that very moment, I realise three important things.

Number one. Drookit is bleeding from a gash in his cheek. It's half-crusted over, but the blood on his fur is unmistakable.

Number two. There is no Bairdy.

Number three, and the most chilling of all. Bairdy's tent is still in its bag, lying exactly where it lay last night, with our leader's backpack beside it, untouched.

A paralysing chill spreads up my back, across my shoulder blades and along my arms before reaching my neck and prickling across the top of my head.

We are alone.

10
War Council

The morning mist has barely lifted, and we sit dotted around on stones, given that the heather is still saturated with dew. This whole conversation is not going the way I expected. In fact, it isn't a conversation at all. It's me talking. And then no one.

'Bairdy's gone,' I say to them. 'No idea where he went, but Drookit has come back, bleeding. We've got no phones. So, what do we do now?'

For a solid minute, no one answers. I have been staring at the ground, but now I dare to lift my head up. *Who is the quiet and subdued boy in front of me and what has he done with the chief loudmouth of the universe, Sorley Mackay? Honestly, the one time you want him to have something to say.*

'Maybe he has come to harm?' Mariam suggests quietly,

never quite taking her eyes off Drookit. I have got him firmly by the collar, but she still doesn't trust that she is safe. I can tell.

'I imagine something hasn't gone right, yeah,' I snap sarcastically. I don't mean to bite off her head like this, but we need a plan, not stupid statements of the obvious.

'Do we go after him?' Rupert suggests, scraping the ground with a stick. For some reason even this irritates me. 'To help?'

I scratch my head, panic rising in my throat. 'What can *we* do? How could *we* offer anything useful? And we don't even know where he is, do we?'

'Would the dog show us?' Rupert replies, keeping his voice even, but I can tell that he is mightily unsettled too.

'He can't be that far away,' Mariam mumbles, but I pretend I haven't heard because I don't think she is necessarily right. I take a deep breath.

Oh my goodness, why am I the one trying to sort this mess out? I am in no way the best person to deal with this. I am in no way the best person to deal with anything. Uninvited, hot tears shoot up in my eyes, but I blink them away before anyone else sees. At least I hope so. *Mum, that's who you want. She is the best person in a crisis. Me? I am the worst. No – probably the second worst, after useless, wordless, gormless Sorley who keeps looking up at the crest of the mountain.*

Finally, I explode. 'Sorley? Anything to contribute here? After all, you're not usually this shy, are you? Spit it out, what should we do, genius?'

Mariam and Rupert's eyes flit up in surprise at the

venom in my voice, but thankfully they don't choose to make a thing of it. I don't think I could handle it. *Breathe, Kenzie!*

To my shock, I think Sorley also seems to concentrate on his breathing. Could the great Sorley Mackay be as terrified as I am?

Rupert stands up. 'All right. Two of us stay here. The other two take the dog and see where he leads. We should all shout for Bairdy. He may have had an accident or got hurt. That way we may find him, but whatever we do, we must not get lost, so don't go too far and keep the camp in sight. Looks like the mist is clearing. Bairdy probably has the good map with him, but I have this.' He holds up a small compass and the tourist map Bairdy gave him. 'Got this from a taster day at orienteering club. It's not pro kit or anything, but it may help us work out where we are and find our way back. Let's limit the time to a couple of hours. If we can't find him, we'll need to think of another plan.'

A wave of relief crashes through my veins – someone else is taking the initiative and I could hug Rupert for it. Well, almost.

'So, who is coming with me?' He says it like a challenge.

Mariam and I look at Sorley, but he is still staring at his feet, not flicking his show-off quiff aside for once.

'I'll stay and guard the tent,' he mumbles.

My mouth falls open.

'I am not going where that dog is,' Mariam adds quickly. She looks at her feet.

I do not believe it. But I better had, because Rupert

stretches his hand out to help me up from my rock – I can barely feel my bum cheeks anymore. 'Right Kenzie? Let's take Drookit and go.'

There is no point in protesting. I shoot Sorley a last despising look, but he hasn't seen – he is scrambling to his feet and walking behind the toilet rocks, so I can't even follow. At least Mariam has the decency to mumble 'Sorry, Kenzie,' as I pass her.

Rupert looks around. 'There is no sign of the dog leash, is there?'

We discuss possibilities but settle on detaching a guy rope from the tent and tying it onto Drookit's collar. Before long we're on our way, with Drookit pulling hard on the string. It cuts into my hand, but we do our best to keep up with him, stumbling on clumps of moss and rocks.

'BAIRDY!' Rupert bellows every few steps.

'BAIRDYYY,' I echo.

Far behind us in the dell by the tents, the faraway voices of our companions repeat our cries. We hear skylark song, Drookit's whining, our own squelching steps across the moor, the rustle of low vegetation in the wind and the splashing of lochan water on rocks. From time to time, a sharp screech overhead alerts us to a passing bird of prey. Rupert tries to educate me and identifies the bird as a hen harrier, but I could not care less right now. *Get me off this mountain.*

The thing we don't hear is a reply from our mountain guide.

Eventually Drookit ceases to pull on his makeshift lead.

Pleadingly, he looks up at us. I cast about.

'BAIRDYYYYYYYY!' I yell with as much ferocity as I can, though the word is carried away by the wind. Straining to listen, I take a step forward onto the rocks, my eyes focused on the horizon.

'Careful!' Rupert shouts as he pulls me back by the shoulder and I'm glad, because beyond the outcrop there is a sudden, steep and stony drop, almost vertical.

I sway.

'Stand there. I'll try to get close enough to take a look,' he offers. His collar flaps wildly in the breeze and his hair blows into his face.

'Are you mad, Rupert? If he is down there, you can't help him. You're half his size!'

I watch, contorting with tension, as Rupert lies flat on the ground and eases himself towards the edge on his stomach.

'Don't worry, I can't fall like this. I'm just going to try and see.'

In the distance, faint calls of 'Bairdy!' pierce the leaden sky. After what feels like an eternity, Rupert pulls back, and I help him to his feet.

He brushes lichen and moss off his trousers and fleece before turning to me.

He shakes his head.

'Nothing. Let's head back.'

11
An Uneasy Alliance

An hour later we all sit in silence around Bairdy's tent, still in its bag. Bairdy's voice hangs in the air, painting word-pictures of the terrifying creatures haunting these glens. I wish my imagination was a whole lot less active. I can practically feel the invisible hand of the Grey Man press on my throat so that I can barely breathe.

'Should we head down the hill to the minibus again?' Sorley suggests, looking only at Rupert.

Rupert shakes his head. 'No, I think the bus will have been picked up already. You saw how godforsaken that place was. There'll be no one there.'

There is a long silence, only punctuated by Drookit's whimpers. I can tell, wherever Bairdy went, Mariam wishes Drookit had joined him. But we are stuck with the dog and his intermittent whining. Sorley has hardly said a word since Bairdy disappeared. Of all the times in the world, this is when I could have put up with someone confident – someone prepared to take the lead. Something I am emphatically, decidedly and definitely NOT keen to do. *Why has he picked today of all days to stop being Sorley?*

I look around.

Rupert is fiddling with his compass and staring at his feet.

Mariam is sitting back with her eyes closed, only opening them warily when Drookit makes a noise.

Sorley grimaces. In any other context, I'd delight in Sorley wearing a satisfyingly sulky face, but when I look closely, it almost makes me think that he is on the verge of tears.

But that can't possibly be true.

I sigh, deeply.

All right. I guess it's me.

'Well, at least there was a road back there. And where there's a road, there may be other cars, and people. If we walk along the road, eventually we're going to find a house – it makes sense.'

I am astounded by how calm and in-charge my voice sounds. Hopefully, the others won't hear the wobble in it. Rupert rises.

'As good a plan as any! And staying here will achieve nothing. What if Bairdy is hurt and needs help? The sooner we make a move the better.' He begins to unpeg the boys' tent and after a long sigh, Sorley pulls himself up and starts to help.

'Erm, I am going to tie Drookit up over here where you are,' I tell the boys. 'Mariam is scared of him,' I add in a whisper.

I stare at Sorley, daring him to laugh, or make a snide comment, or roll his eyes, or *be Sorley* in any other way. I nearly keel over when he responds, 'Fair enough, cool.' I attach the guy rope to the dog's collar again and wind the other end around a rock by Rupert's backpack.

Mariam and I get to work. Soon our makeshift camp is stored in our bags once more. We don't talk much – it's like there is an unspoken agreement that we need to hear Bairdy, should he call for help. But there's nothing more than the whistling of the wind, the screeches and croaks of the birds and the occasional rustle of something or other in the undergrowth.

'What should we do with Bairdy's tent? And all this?' Sorley gestures at the backpack and our leader's waterproof jacket.

Mariam and I exchange a look. 'Leave it?' I venture, hesitating. 'We can't carry all of this over the hills, can we?'

Mariam says something.

'What?' *I wish she'd speak up.*

'I think we should feed the dog. He'll be hungry.'

The rest of us look at each other – *how did none of us think of that?* I feel bad rummaging through Bairdy's backpack, but there's nothing for it. Thankfully, he seems to have wrapped up portions of dry dog food in individual little bags, as if one was intended for each meal. There is even a metal bowl in there, with cheesy swirly writing of *Best Dog Ever* on it.

'Looks rank!' comments Sorley, sounding much more like himself, but he has the grace to distract the dog while Mariam and I undo the knot in the food bag and place the filled bowl on the ground. Mariam jumps out of the way as Drookit hurls himself at the food, but even she can't help smiling at his enthusiastic wolfing down of something that, let's be honest, looks like cardboard. Once the bowl is empty, Mariam fills it with water from her own bottle. The dog drinks greedily.

'I thought you were scared of the dog!'

Yep, that's the Sorley I recognise, sneering from the sidelines. I am about to give him a piece of my mind when Mariam responds herself, quiet, but determined.

'Yes. I am, Sorley. I'm terrified, and I'm not proud of it. But I do not want to be like this for the rest of my life, so I'm trying, okay?'

I glare at him to avoid another supposedly comedic comeback, but he shows uncharacteristic restraint, goodness knows how. Then he mumbles 'Good for you' which doesn't even sound sarcastic, and slowly begins to walk.

'Time to go, Drookit,' I say in as calm a voice as I can muster. I tuck the spare dog food and the bowl into my pack, along with the camping stove, some food, lighter fluid and matches. We leave Bairdy's tent and bag where we found them – just in case he does return and needs shelter. Finally, together, we search for the path along which we came.

Upsettingly, this proves much harder than I expected.

'Look – footprints – that must have been us.'

'I'm not sure that's a footprint at all …'

'I remember that bit of water. It was on our right. Bairdy called it a lochan, didn't he?'

'Well, there is another one of those. And another one over there, see it? Which one was it?'

'Erm …'

It isn't long before I'm not sure I recognise anything anymore. It's as if the mountain peaks have mischievously rearranged themselves just to fool us.

Perhaps this is the magic of the Grey Man of Ben MacDui, to lure us to his lair …

Oh, stop it Kenzie!

I wish I could mute my imagination, just until I get home.

'Careful!' Rupert shouts, but it's too late – the ground has suddenly become a marshy peatbog and my boots sink in almost as far as my ankle.

'Move back,' I warn as I let go of the dog to free myself. It takes all my self-control to keep the shake of panic out of my voice. Mariam has placed each of her feet on a clump of moss and reaches over to help. But however hard I stretch my hands out, I cannot reach her.

'Don't go in as far as I have, Mariam. It helps no one if both of us are stuck.'

In answer she retreats and casts about. With a small cry of triumph, she returns with a sapling as long as my leg, likely of the kind that don't survive long because of all the deer as Bairdy said yesterday. That feels like an eternity ago now. 'Kenzie, focus. Here, grab this.'

I hold on to the bendy wood with all my might. Rupert has found another stick. I grip that too with my other hand, and with a giant squelch, the peat gives up my boots. I move my legs as fast as I can until I reach drier ground again. Sorley is standing by at a distance, his forehead knotted into a tight frown.

'I don't like the look of those clouds,' he comments.

'Well, I'm a little more concerned about the fact that I nearly lost my boots in that quagmire, which would not have been fun, Sorley Mackay. I'll deal with your forecast of doom later, weatherman!'

It is only when I inspect the damage to my shoes (my *new* shoes, which Mum and Granny bought with good money they don't really have) that I realise how tense my torso is. It takes a conscious effort to breathe, and my heart pounds like a woodpecker.

'Glad you're okay, Kenzie,' Rupert mumbles and I give him a grateful smile. 'But guys …' He points. We follow. And right enough, a few yards from where I was stuck a minute ago is Drookit.

Or what remains visible of him: his head, bits of his back. The tip of his tail. His eyes are white with fear. He whines pleadingly.

Sorley swears.

The rest of Drookit is submerged in dark brown peaty mud.

The dog is stuck.

And worse, he knows it.

12
Stuck

'Drookit! Stop thrashing around! You'll only sink in deeper!'

I know, I know – I am getting irritated, but all attempts to soothe the dog have failed. Sorley and Rupert have run to a nearby clump of trees to see if they can find anything that could help. Mariam, however, has another idea.

'Rocks – we need to find rocks and make a bridge out of them. Stepping stones, do you get it? A bridge over to the dog.'

'That's a lot of rocks, Mariam!'

She groans helplessly. 'Have you got a better idea, Kenzie?'

I do not.

'So then help me.' She lifts a round-shaped rock and

carefully lowers it between three clumps of reedy grass, wedging it into place. 'There. Now another.'

By the time the boys return with a pair of gnarled branches, we are more than halfway towards the dog. He is moving less now, but we all know he's only getting tired. I stop myself from thinking the thought which logically follows.

'He is sinking, guys, we need to be quick. Shall we try? Now?' Rupert looks around. 'Who is going to do it?'

Sorley shrugs. 'Makes sense for the lightest people to do it.'

Mariam and I exchange a glance. 'Are you up for it?' I ask.

She shrugs. I take that as a yes and gently lower my weight onto the stones – one step at a time. She follows. I use a branch to steady myself and distribute my weight more widely. Once we reach the dog, I lower the branch across the muddy gap and turn. 'We can't stand here long; we have to be fast. You reach in and take a front paw, and I'll take the other. Then we both pull. Hopefully he'll kick with his hind legs and come free. Right?'

I want out of this quagmire, out of these mountains, out of this group, away from here.

'Let's go. Ready. Steady ...'

I sink to my knees onto the twigs and branches as mud squelches through. Trying to ignore the cloying smell of the peat, I roll up my sleeves and plunge my hands into the mire to grab for Drookit's front leg. 'Got one! Go Mariam!'

I hear her hiss an angry word under her breath, but to her credit she does as I ask. I feel Drookit's tongue on my upper arms as we heave.

'Harder!' I bite my lip as I strain. 'HARDER, Mariam, pull! Drookit, come ON!'

With an enormous effort, the mud-soaked body of the dog comes free, and he scampers past us and across our makeshift safety bridge towards the boys where he shakes himself heartily, spraying mud and black-brown water over them both as Mariam and I retreat to join them.

'Drookit! You minger!'

Despite the seriousness of our situation, I can't help laughing at Sorley's protest, setting free some of the tension we must all feel.

It is Rupert who reminds us of our real task. 'So, guys, any idea where the road is? No fibbing!'

We look around. 'Honestly, no.' I admit.

Sorley and Mariam answer with shrugs.

Sorley was right – the clouds have descended, hiding anything beyond middle-distance from view.

I take a deep breath. 'When Bairdy was here, he did point to that ridge there, didn't he? Didn't he say there was a village on the other side?'

All heads follow my outstretched arm – even the dog's.

'And no one expects us back by the road anyway. Think about it: even if we found it, it would be miles and miles before we'd get to any sort of town – the drive took ages, right? At least we have a direction for that village – let's find it and ask for help there. Apart from anything else, it makes sense to go up so we can see as far as possible.' I finish with a flourish, probably sounding much more confident than I actually feel: 'Let's head up, not down.'

I feel a sudden surge of exhaustion after that big speech.

No one contradicts me, although I see a strange shadow cross Sorley's face. Mariam nods.

Rupert agrees: 'Well, if the weather continues like this, we need to make as much progress as we can. With this low cloud it's possible that the higher we go, the more we'll see. We might get above the clouds, and if the weather clears and there really is a village nearby, we'll spot it from above. Good plan, Kenzie.'

We feed Drookit a few pieces from his next food bag and give him another drink, this time from my water bottle.

And then there is nothing for it: shouldering our packs again, we set off towards the towering peaks, hiding and re-emerging from banks of low cloud. Before long, most of the colours disappear altogether. A chill settles on us as we begin our ascent into the greying world of the peaks above us.

Up.

Up.

Up.

Half an hour's walking, and the drizzle begins. Soon we squelch and slide with every step, and Rupert, who is carrying the bulk of the tents, stops every few steps to catch his breath. At first, I was able to convince myself that there was a path of some sort. But now we are weaving our way upwards in wide zigzags, turning back on ourselves whenever we hit an unexpectedly boggy stretch, or when we inadvertently stumble upon a steep drop. Sorley keeps at the back of the group, a marked change to his racing Rupert at the start. One thing is certain though – none of us are in a talkative mood. Each of us keeps our own counsel. I have nothing to say, and even if I had, I am too out of breath to say it. The incline becomes steeper. Finally, the leaden sky above us splits open to reveal an ocean of cloud spread out beneath us, with the peaks surfacing like islands beneath the fiery ball sinking slowly in the sky.

'Guys, I don't think we should walk any further,' Rupert puffs at last. He looks almost green with exertion. 'I can't carry this thing anymore, and let's face it, we're not making much headway anyway. Plus, it'll take us a bit of time to set up camp again, especially if we don't have … anyone to help us. That little spring was only five minutes ago, wasn't it? So, we can boil water from that.'

'Fair enough,' Sorley adds, just a little bit too readily for my liking.

Wouldn't it be best to push on a little more? The very next little summit may reveal something encouraging, like a village, or a rescue helicopter, or a burger restaurant…

'I think the boys are right. Let's set up the tents,' Mariam sighs. She too has been carrying a tent while I took charge of Drookit on our ascent. Our tent bag, though lightweight, crashes onto the ground.

'Careful!' I snap. 'Can't break the tent poles or we're

doomed.' I pause. 'Actually, we're doomed anyway.'

'Cheery language, Kenzie. Great for morale, well done. Just what everyone needs.'

Yep, that's the sarky, nasty, irritating bully that I remember. The real Sorley is back.

'Shut up Sorley,' I hiss under my breath.

Mariam and Rupert are ignoring us, getting on with wrestling tent pegs into the stony ground. I take myself away to clear a space for the stove like Bairdy did. His nifty little camping cooker just fitted into my bag, and I retrieve it now, closing my eyes to visualise how Bairdy made our hot chocolate yesterday – pouring a little of the bright pink liquid into the bottom part, adding the holed cover and lighting the flame with Bairdy's lighter. *Phew, it seems to be working.* Sorley wandered back to the spring to fetch water and returns with a full camping pot. Thankfully the wind has dropped for now. Wordlessly, he hands me the container and I begin to boil the pasta we took from Bairdy's supplies.

It is through the steam from the pot that I spot it, only for a moment, high on the hill before us, sharply outlined against the darkening sky.

A figure. Tall, lean, looming.

We are not alone.

13
Night Wandering

'It could be Bairdy, couldn't it? Maybe he's injured? Or confused,' Rupert volunteers.

'OR, it could be the Grey Man of Ben MacDui,' adds Sorley in a mock-trembling voice, immature enough to make me want to hit him, push him, slap him and kick him at the same time.

I roll my eyes at Mariam instead and she responds by doing the same. I feel better at once.

'If it's not Bairdy, then who could it be?' Mariam mumbles.

I shrug. 'Remember Bairdy saw someone up there not long after we set off? Whoever that was.'

There is silence.

'Should we go and see?' I finally add. 'Just to make sure?'

'What, now?' Sorley snorts. 'It's almost dark. You're off your head.'

I glare at Sorley. He glares at me. The other two exchange a glance too, probably wondering why the two of us are constantly at each other's throats, but it's Sorley's fault for being an idiot, and I am not sorry. Just at that very moment it begins to rain. First isolated drops, which turn into millions of drops, which turn into a deluge.

Mariam reacts first: 'Quick! The food!'

The camping stove has already gone out. Just as well I drained the pasta and added the sauce, closing the lid. At least it's lukewarm. Mariam holds the flap of her raincoat over me as I shovel the portions into the lightweight camping bowls and all but throw two of them at the boys. They speedily retreat into the entrance of their tent where they crouch, bedraggled, and begin eating. I cover the stove with the upturned cooking pot and follow Mariam to our own tent, the weight of layers and layers of wet fabric sticking to my skin. A sharp gust of wind almost blows the food into my face. Unfortunately for me, it also carries snippets of Sorley's speech over to us.

'... telling you, Kenzie is off her head! Always has been ...'

I watch Rupert shrug in the distance, and my eyes begin to sting.

Then I feel Mariam's elbow to my side. 'Ignore him. I think Sorley is being mean to you. There's no need for it.'

She doesn't look up from her food, and I am grateful, because one or two tears may just have escaped my eyes and are pooling with the raindrops on the rims of my bowl. Despite the creeping cold, and the damp rising through every layer of my clothing, a shy kind of warmth spreads through my chest.

Mariam is on my side.

We do not reconvene that night. As I've been the one carrying the dog food, Drookit sleeps between the outer and inner layers of our tent, and Mariam does not even complain. Just before I turn in, I step outside one last time. My torchlight illuminates a thousand trickles from the sky. The top of the mountain is shrouded in mist. Clouds hide the moon, too. There will be no chance of spotting a figure on the summit, although if I listen really, really hard, there is a moaning – a wheezy groaning on the breeze. *Did I imagine it? Could my brain play such tricks on me? In fact, did I imagine the hunched figure earlier? Or ...* I shudder once more. *What if there really is a Grey Man?*

I'm not proud of it, but I run the last few steps back to our tent, relieved that the next time I emerge it'll be daylight and our ordeal will be over, one way or the other. We will fail to appear at the collection point as expected, and the process will kick in. People will search for us. Tomorrow will be the day we are rescued, discovered, or find our way. Whatever it is, it will be over. And then Sorley can crawl back into the hole from which he came, and I can read in my room, tidy up the library shelves at school, use big words and keep my own company. Things will be back as they should be.

Won't they?

It is a restless night. Mariam shivers beside me, Drookit whines every time we turn, and the rain tears at our tent without mercy.

The early hours yield even less sleep. Whenever I open my eyes, Mariam seems to lie in a different position.

'Are you okay?' I venture. The answer is a snore.

I turn away again and think it all through. *No one expects us back before this afternoon. No one will raise the alarm until then. But I can't stop wondering – what if the figure I saw up on the mountain needs help? What if it really was our missing mountain guide? He could have lost his memory. Maybe he banged his head, or is so dehydrated he's hallucinating or something?*

Guilt nibbles at my conscience.

I feel bad not going to look.

My stomach pulls itself into a knot as I have an unspoken argument with myself.

What, now?
When else?
Alone?
What choice do I have?
Sorley is right, you really are off your head!

It's madness – the cold first light is only just icing the top of the hills to the east, but I sit up, pull off the cold-sticky sleeping bag, wriggle my trousers over my pyjamas and pull on two, no, *three* tops. The tent zip is stiff, but I manage to undo it and slowly, my eyes get used to the gloom outside.

'Not far,' I whisper to myself. 'Just enough to get a view.

Stay here, boy.'

Drookit lays himself down once more, his tail still wagging intermittently, as if he knows – this is a girl's mission, and a solo one. Sealing our tent once more, I strike out upwards, past clumps of bog cotton and rocks glistening with damp. The tops of the surrounding hills are alight now, pink fire fading into the sky. The moon is still there, but paling, and the further I walk, the more I see. Even if I had need of it, I do not think I would use my torch. Something inside my crowded mind would forbid it. A sense of foreboding perhaps? *Foreboding*? Gosh, thank goodness Sorley isn't here to make fun of my word choice. He would call it pompous if he had the vocabulary to do it.

Everything grows close to the ground up here, dry heather crunching with every step. From time to time a mountain hare bounds along the hillside or nibbles its breakfast. The camp drops below me as I gain more and more perspective. Until something strange catches my eye. Just ahead, on the ground. I hesitate and narrow my eyes.

What IS that? Reluctantly, I approach.

Whatever it is, it's a mighty, feathered mess.

I carefully give it a nudge with my foot. It is a large bird, with a reddish-brown tummy, white, black-tipped wings, and a hooked beak. On closer inspection, it is stiff. Cold.

And also, dead.

Very dead.

'And finally, Kenzie stops,' a familiar and dreaded voice behind me snaps. I give a jump and a mini scream at the same time, thankfully obscured by the wind. *Flipping*

Sorley Mackay! The very last person on earth I would choose for company.

'Sorley! You scared me. What are you doing here?'

He gestures, his arms wide. 'That question is rich coming from you! *You* went off up the hill on your own. I couldn't sleep so I thought I'd have a look, if there was any sign of the man you were on about – but then I spotted *you* instead, heading away. I did call after you, but you didn't hear me, so I had to run after you, didn't I!'

'Oh, shut up, Sorley, I was never going to go far. But then I saw this.' I gesture at the mess on the ground.

Sorley's face wrinkles. Then, for reasons best known to Sorley, he fumbles in his jacket pocket to take a pic on his disposable camera. Click. He holds his nose and takes a step backwards from the bird on the ground. 'Eugh, it stinks. Doesn't look like it's been here all that long though. Why are its claws so curled up?'

'Dunno,' I shrug. 'But your picture probably won't show anything – I don't think it's bright enough. I wonder if this bird has anything to do with the person I saw earli–'

Sorley's head snaps sideways and back to me. 'Shhhh!' He's almost spitting in his urgency. 'Listen!'

The very next moment he grabs my sleeve, pulls me down into the heather and crawls towards a large rock nearby, dragging me behind him.

'SORLEY, let go!' I hiss. 'If that's an adult, then we need to speak to them. We need help, in case you haven't noticed, you idiot!'

'Oh, my goodness. Shut up Kenzie! Whoever it is, that

isn't Bairdy, and we don't know if we can trust whoever is up here this early in the morning.'

Grudgingly I have to admit that he has a point. Why would a sane adult be out here at this time? The Grey Man crunches into my mind, but I usher the monster right out again. I can't afford to be distracted right now.

Sorley elbows me extra hard to emphasise his point, so finally I comply, curling myself into a tight ball. The heather prickles painfully on my throat, but I press my face sideways into the undergrowth: to see, without *being* seen.

However, what I see takes my breath away – and not in a good way.

A wince of fear emanates from Sorley, crouching somewhere close beside me.

He has seen it too.

The cold glint of muted light on metal.

The metal barrel of a shotgun in the stranger's hands.

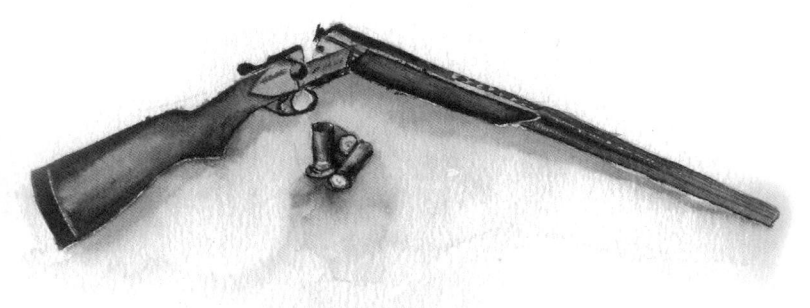

14
The Cold Glint of Metal

We press ourselves deeper into the heather, wriggling as low into the vegetation as we can. I scrunch up my eyes for good measure, although I don't know what this will achieve. How stupid we were to set off on our own! Somewhere down that hillside, Mariam and Rupert are sleeping in their tents, none the wiser at all. And what about Bairdy? What if he has come to harm from this armed stranger? I hold my breath.

We can hear the man breathing, rasping with the effort, but sure-footed too. I wonder if he is an older person. Then another set of crunching, squelching steps approaches – we squeeze down harder. I can't see a thing now, but if one of them has a gun the other one may be armed too. I wait for them to speak, but they do not.

Instead, there is a crinkle of plastic. I risk lifting my head a little – a smaller, stockier man is wrestling the dead bird into a bag with gloved hands. There is thick writing on the bag. *Agricultural Fertiliser*, I think it says.

I feel Sorley wriggle beside me. What is he doing? *Stay still!*

Of course I can't actually say it, however quietly. I see his hand stretching out beyond our stone. *Sorley, you're mad! Whatever you're doing, stop it!* And then I see: his small disposable camera is in his hand. He points it and clicks, twice. Each sound shoots through me like an electric shock. *Surely, they will hear! Surely, they will see.* By now I am absolutely certain that we're witnessing a crime. I had always thought it would be exciting to be there when a crime was committed. Right now, I wish I was anywhere else, anywhere but here – anywhere but the mountains.

And then the terrible realisation hits me – *if Bairdy saw what we are seeing. If he heard what we are hearing. It would be just like him to challenge the men. And if he did … oh no …*

They have a gun. They have a gun a gun a gun a gun …

I can feel my breaths coming faster and faster, and then I can't control them anymore.

"Shh Kenzie!' Sorley hisses.

'Wait! What was that?' The rasping voice of a man, not three yards away from us on the other side of the rock.

We hear rustling on the ground.

'Probably a pine marten,' a much younger voice replies. 'Let's get out of here. It would be just our luck to bump into another damn climber.'

The old man barely replies, answering in a simple grunt. I hear the clicking of metal as he plays with his trigger.

The strangers walk right past our rock but turn away in the opposite direction from our tents, barely visible in the distant mist. Drizzle comes and goes, but Sorley and I do not move. Not for a long, long, long time.

'Are they gone, do you think?' I ask at last. My hand is still firmly pressed over my mouth so my hyperventilating won't give us away.

'Think so,' my enemy answers.

Detangling our clammy bodies feels like unfolding a pair of particularly convoluted paper aeroplanes – ones that will never fly again. The weather is clearing.

'Can you still see them, Kenzie?'

I cannot. But the morning light illuminates the ground half-heartedly. I stretch and rise slowly.

'Sorley, look! Oh no.'

We turn our attention to where the dead animal lay when we first arrived. Traces of feathers still stick in the undergrowth. But on a low smooth rock nearby lies a fresh slab of stinking meat – a dead hare, disgustingly cut open, its innards exposed and sprinkled with dark blue granules. I suppress a retch. Sorley bends down to take a closer look, but I yank him back sharply.

'NO! Careful, that'll be toxic. Those guys collected the dead bird – the evidence, if you like. And now they've left this bait to poison other raptors. It's sick!'

Sorley wrinkles his nose in disgust, but to my surprise,

his eyes are brimming. 'Oh man, imagine! What if Drookit ate meat like that?'

'Exactly. We must get rid of it before another animal dies.'

Sorley looks around helplessly. 'But how?'

I think for a moment. 'Okay … okay … how about you take a photo of it all, before we touch anything. Then we should bury the meat so no other animal will suffer like that poor bird earlier.'

Moments later, we are shovelling mud and clammy earth with our bare hands, digging a sloshing hole which immediately fills with peaty water from the ground below. We use sticks to lift the poisoned bait in a pincer motion and drop it into the pit before filling it with more mud, placing a heavy rock on top for good measure.

'That should do it.' Sorley grunts with satisfaction, holding his muddy hand up for a high five before remembering that it's me who is here with him. I have already high-fived it before remembering that this is in fact Sorley Mackay's hand. Both of us smile in embarrassment before quickly dunking our hands into a puddle nearby.

'Probably full of bugs,' I say to break the awkward silence.

'Yep, definitely,' he answers. 'I've got sanitiser in the tent. I can give you some.'

My shoulders stay clenched and tense, right until we reach the two small tents tucked into the shelter of the mountainside. Only when I unzip the entrance to the tent and Mariam stirs in her sleep and opens her eyes do I begin to believe that we got away with it: the armed men did not see us. All is on track – a search party will be on the way before we know it.

I try to block all thoughts of Bairdy from my mind.

He is an adult. He is a mountain guide. He knows what he's doing, right? And even if something had happened to him, we would be in no position to help. We need to concentrate on surviving, and now there is a new responsibility too. We need to tell people what we saw up there. Collect evidence, keep our eyes open. Who knows what these men will do when they realise their bait has been tampered with?

Oh, my goodness, that's just it.

While we are here, we're as dangerous to those men as they are to us.

We need to get down from this mountain.

15
Of Earth and Sky

I'll say it for Rupert and Mariam: they believe us at once. Both of them, despite sleeping through Sorley's and my early morning excursion, rise to the challenge. The tents are packed and stacked in less than twenty minutes, and no one even mentions food – unless you count Drookit who prods and whines and paws us all until someone thinks to give him his ration. He wags his tail and gulps it down, and I wonder how he eats that stuff – it looks more revolting than dry Weetabix. It doesn't seem to bother him much. He still looks around as if Bairdy is going to emerge from the mist at any minute, but he also wags his tail whenever any of us come near. We are his pack now, and I feel extra motivated to look after him. Mariam has begun to stroke his head, behind the ears where he likes it the most, and he licks her hand. She pulls it away with a yelp, but Sorley reassures her. 'It's what dogs do when they like someone – like a kiss from your mum or something.'

I string the guy rope to he dog's collar once more and we are away.

'Kenzie, what did the bird look like? The dead one you found?'

Rupert has caught up with me.

'What does it matter? It was big. Reddish brown with white and a bit of black on the wings. Yellow and black beak.'

'A red kite then, you think?'

'How should I know, Rupert?'

He ignores my rudeness. 'I have heard of this sort of thing before, Kenzie. Birds of prey are often targeted and killed. Shooting estates try to protect their grouse stock and make sure that raptors don't hunt them. And if a gamekeeper puts out poison, they may kill the eagles and buzzards they are after, but they may also hurt those which mostly scavenge, like kites. It's illegal, of course, but most of the time they get away with it. Animals can't talk, and with areas like this,' – he gestures towards the sweeping mountainsides and endless moors – 'there are usually no witnesses. It's really hard to get convictions. My dad is in the police, and he has a colleague who deals with this stuff.'

'Well, I hope your dad's pal can sort this out. Personally, the library is my preferred habitat – but these hills should be safe for the creatures that naturally live here. It's going to be hard to prove anything, though, we didn't even catch those men's names. Who knows where they came from.'

He nods thoughtfully. 'But you did witness it, two of you. And Sorley even took some photos, didn't he? Maybe there is a chance after all. I think you were both mad to set out at that time without telling us, but maybe it'll work out for the best.'

An unspoken thought rises like a wall between us. A Bairdy-shaped silence. What has happened to our leader? Is he alive? Will it make a difference to him whether we get out of these hills quickly or not? And is it too late?

Neither of us can answer these questions, so we don't even raise them. Instead, we traipse onwards, upwards, across rivulets and rocks, up gulleys and scrambling up scree. Upwards towards the ridge. On the other side, we hope, our pickup point awaits. It will be over. I am propelled along by those words as I repeat them again and again in my head. It will be over. Get across the ridge. It will be over. Get across the ridge.

Soon the hillside is so steep that we have to stop to catch our breath every few steps. Even Sorley, who has been more of his usual talkative self, retelling our dawn encounter in ever more dramatic versions, has settled down a little. We reach a small natural platform and Mariam – who is the smallest and slightest of us – calls a halt. 'Guys. I can't go on just now. Can we take a break?'

Gratefully I throw down my backpack, giving Drookit a fright in the process. I sink down beside my tent-mate and lean back against the hillside. My eyes close with exhaustion, but as soon as I open them again, something odd happens. Odd and wonderful and unexpected.

'Woooooow.'

Yes, it was me who said it. Which isn't like me.

It is as if the whole world has been touched by golden magic. Dark clouds churn and stir overhead. Bright rays of sunlight battle through and throw gold dust over the undulating hillside. I can't believe how high we have climbed! It's hard to even spot where our tents were pitched last night. Earth and sky sing the same song, lochans reflect the clouds and the heavens echo the greys, browns and blues of the shadows on the hills. Rupert points at a herd of deer on the opposite hillside. Two stags with their sharply outlined antlers stand guard at the top while scores more animals blend into the vegetation lower down.

'Did you know that there are— ' Rupert begins.

'A million deer in Scotland,' we all echo before remembering who mentioned that particular fact only two days ago. Yes, we are still stranded up here. But somehow, I don't mind it the same, here where the landscape spreads out beneath us like a page in a book, patterned with patches of trees, rivers and springs, lochans and a wild, harsh, singing beauty. I find it difficult to get my head around it. What a place. What a country. What a privilege to be here, right now, and see the ever-changing patterns on the ground, and the soaring shapes of birds above us, so high I can barely see them circle.

'Eagles,' mumbles Rupert beside me and nudges me,

handing me his miniscule pair of binoculars. 'Take a look.'

I do. It takes me a while to find the birds through the small viewfinder, but once I have one, I follow its majestic glide. It barely flaps its wings – in fact it does not. It simply soars and glides and rides the thermals, or that's what Rupert calls it.

'Here Mariam, you have a look too.'

My friend looks up through the binoculars. 'We get really large eagles in Pakistan as well, when we visit my family. They live in the mountains too. It can take almost a day to get to the next village.'

All three of us look sharply across. 'You've done this sort of walk before?' Sorley asks.

'Trekking? Yes – although usually with a guide, and donkeys to carry the heaviest loads. Wish I had a donkey now,' she quips, giving a mournful look in the direction of our heavy packs. I laugh.

'Could try Drookit,' I suggest, earning me a belly-laugh from the group and a whine of outrage from the dog – don't tell me he understood that!

'I know we are in a bit of a situation just now, but it is amazing up here, isn't it,' says Rupert, scanning the landscape once more as he rises for the final push to the top.

Mariam and I join him, with Sorley going last. He has become a lot quieter again. I spot him biting his lip as he finally shoulders his backpack and straps it into place.

'Let's go then,' he snaps through gritted teeth.

The final part of the way is steep, although parts of it

look like a path again, which gives us some reassurance. We can't have gone entirely wrong then – and Bairdy did point this way, I'm sure. As we follow the rockface, the path levels out and shrinks to a narrow ledge, no wider than the length of my arm. As I approach it, the ground falls away on both sides before the path broadens again. *Yikes. Concentrate, Kenzie!*

'Keep going Mariam,' I encourage her over my shoulder. 'But watch out – there is a bit of a drop coming up here, thankfully not for long. Careful!'

However, it isn't Mariam I need to worry about.

16
Sorley's Secret

Sorley has slowed to a halt and is eyeing the ground beneath our feet with suspicion. He's mumbling to himself, but we can't make it out.

'Mate, come on,' tries Rupert. His voice is gentle, but I detect a little tremble of panic in it.

What's wrong with the most annoying boy in the history of my school, the history of my country and probably the world?

His feet have not moved – all he does is stare. Stare down.

To be fair, it is a slope to end all slopes. The ridge narrows across it before widening onto the plateau on the other side.

'Erm, guys ...' Sorley has turned a tense shade of white. 'Guys, I don't think I can do it.' His voice is barely audible now. 'I'm sorry, but I just can't. You're going to have to go without me.'

As if to lend weight to his statement, the wind picks up and our jackets flutter hard. With a pathetic whimper, Sorley sinks to his knees. He has actually closed his eyes.

The rest of us look at each other. Drookit rubs it in by scampering backwards and forwards across the narrow walkway, sniffing excitedly.

'Sorley, come on man,' Rupert tries. He sounds exhausted, as if scraping for the last of the butter in an empty dish. 'We need to get down from here. You know that.'

My arch-enemy does not respond. He opens his eyes a chink, peeks down the abyss for a millisecond and scrunches them tight again. 'Guys, I am sorry,' he finally answers, his voice unnaturally high. 'I mean it. I've never been that good with heights, but this … this is definitely not something I can do. Sorry,' he repeats one last time as if that made everything all right.

I am not sure what comes over me, but something snaps, like a rubber band stretched too tight. I am screeching. 'For goodness' sake, Sorley! Honestly, you talk the tallest of tales, but now? Now you are actually going to let us down. The longer we have to wait for you here, the more danger we are in. You saw the guys with their guns! The weather is awful. I am soaked and sodden and SICK of your attention seeking. Get across that path or so help me I'll push you down that slope myself. I mean it. I wouldn't even feel bad, the way you've made me feel every minute of my school life.'

Subtly, I feel a gentle touch on my arm. Mariam has leant over. 'Leave it, Kenzie. This isn't helping anyone.' She turns, even though the wind has picked up and whips her loose strands of hair right into her face. 'Sorley,' she cajoles him smoothly. 'You can definitely do this. I'm coming for you, and we'll do it together. You can get across, it's only a few metres. Honestly, it's less tricky than it looks. The three of us are already across – and this bit is the worst part of the path. Look over there? The path gets wider going forward, doesn't it?'

Sorley lifts his face, and I can see the remains of tears crusting on his cheeks. It actually looks as if he is struggling to breathe. I feel a stab of guilt in my stomach – *I shouldn't have been so mean to him. Truth be told, the way I have been talking, I am no better than him, just as nasty and ready to exploit his weakness as he has been with me. Just as vile.* I take a big breath.

'Yeah, I'm coming too. I'll carry your pack across – that might help.'

Rupert looks up in surprise as I cast my own bag to the ground. Without it, I feel suddenly featherlight – but also wobbly on my feet. After a moment to adjust, I set off, determined not to be infected by Sorley's dread. *A step forward ... and then another ...*

I make it across and carefully sidestep Sorley who is still crouching on the ground, staring at his feet. Mariam is right behind me. She slides the straps of the backpack off Sorley and takes his hand. 'Come on, Sorley. If I can do it, anyone can. You are much taller and heavier than me. And sportier, probably. Just look across, don't allow yourself to look down. If that was the wall outside the library in town, you could balance on it no problem. In fact, this is wider than that wall, isn't it? Now, forget about the drop. It's just a wall, that's all it is.' Her soothing voice drips with magic, I am sure of it. I allow Sorley's backpack to tip towards me and heave it onto my own shoulders. Then I watch as Mariam coaxes the boy to his feet and leads him, step by small step, across the narrow stretch, with Rupert shouting encouragement from the other side. Once Sorley gets near, Rupert holds his hand out for Sorley to grasp. Sorley hesitates and it looks as if he's going to freeze altogether, trapping Mariam and me on the ridge.

'Come on Sorley, you're so close. You're doing brilliantly!' The words are out of my own mouth before I realise what I'm doing. And maybe it's what he needed, because at that moment, he speeds his steps and scrambles across, until Rupert grasps his arm and pulls him over to where the ground flattens out.

'Woohoo, look, you've DONE IT!' Mariam cheers, patting Sorley on the shoulder. He's sunk to his knees once more, watching anxiously as I balance my way across one last time, weighed down with his heavy pack. I sink against the cliff-face beside him, panting hard and wriggling the heavy bag off my back.

Rupert looks relieved. 'Okay, team, back on track. Take a minute Sorley. You too, Kenzie. Great work everyone. Mariam, does that bit down there look like a proper path to you? Tell you what, why don't the two of us check it out.

We can leave our packs here with yours while you rest for a bit. We'll be back soon.'

Both Sorley and I look up sharply.

Rupert grins. 'We won't be long, don't worry, guys. But I get it, best not to set out on our own now. I know what you mean.'

Sorley and I exchange a glance. Then we remember who we are and look away quickly. Rupert and Mariam add their backpacks to ours, forming a prison wall around us, and carefully pick their way towards the area Rupert pointed at earlier.

And I am left with Sorley Mackay.

17
Truce

I let my eyes drift to the middle distance. The hills around the horizon look almost purple now, with one or two slashes of white snow, and veils of mist drifting along and across them. Down in the glen, lochans still reflect the intermittent light, some dark and unfathomable and others on fire with golden sunlight. Lifting my eyes, I follow the movements of a bird, circling high above us, wings outstretched. Hang on, are there two? I think so. Drookit has curled up by my feet, taking a chance to rest too, and I find that my hand travels to stroke his matted fur all of its own accord.

'I think those two may be eagles too,' croaks Sorley, and I'm so surprised at his tone I can't help looking at him. He looks nothing like himself – thinner somehow, and younger. One of his eyelids keeps twitching. I nod and look up again, but Sorley starts once more. Sorley Mackay is choosing to talk to me!

'Look, Kenzie …'

He runs out of steam but begins again.

'Kenzie, that was, erm, nice of you. To help me with my pack like that.'

Goodness, I don't know how to respond to this. What's happening?

'Erm, that's okay,' I eventually venture. Mariam and Rupert have shrunk into the distance but appear to have stopped.

'Kenzie, I've always been like this, with high places. To be honest, I tried everything I could to get out of this trip.' Sorley looks at his feet, despite the eagles above and the postcard view below us.

'Me too! I even pretended to be ill,' I splutter before cursing myself for letting my guard down. But Sorley doesn't take advantage of my moment of weakness. Instead, he looks up, his face vexed.

'You didn't want to come because of me, right?'

I hadn't expected this.

All right. We're really doing this, are we? I inhale slowly before choosing my words. 'Yes, I suppose – if I'm honest. Not *just* because of you though.'

Sorley nods, the breeze teasing at his quiff. 'But mainly. And I can see why.'

I shift uncomfortably. I don't know how to deal with this Sorley. The usual Sorley, I can just ignore or avoid, as best I can. This Sorley is human.

'Look Kenzie, I know I've given you a hard time over

the years, and you are nowhere near as stuck up as I thought you were. So, I'm really sorry, okay? I'm a bit loud, I guess, and always have been. But you – you are always so brainy, and it's hard for the rest of us sometimes when you find everything so easy.'

I actually laugh at that. 'I am NOT finding *this* easy!'

Sorley begins a cautious smile. 'That makes two of us then.'

There is a long pause as we both try to retrace the birds in the clouds above. Drookit gives a little twitch in his daydream and wags his tail. I wonder what he is imagining right now. Meanwhile, I think back to some of my interactions with Sorley throughout school. The more I think about them, the less comfortable I become. 'I'm not all that brainy,' I finally say, but he snorts in response.

I try again. 'All right. Whatever you think, I can see that I haven't exactly been kind to you either. Sorry if I've made you feel stupid, Sorley.'

'You read all the time – no wonder you're clever. I find reading really hard.'

Now, to this I do have an answer. 'You should try audiobooks. The library has some brilliant ones, like …' I trail off, because the full force of it has just hit me like a baseball bat to the stomach: the library is my safe place. This mountain top is the exact opposite. For the first time I wonder whether I will ever see the library again.

'Look, the others are coming back.' He looks across at me, his face a little less grey. This time he holds my gaze, as if he is finally certain of something again. 'Can we call it a truce, Kenzie? Just for this trip? Or, like, longer if you like. If there's another steep bit, I may need someone to coax me across again. Honestly, why am I like this!'

I giggle before declaring firmly: 'Fine, it's a deal. A truce is all right with me.'

There is no shaking of hands or clapping on the shoulder, like you see in the movies. We simply stretch our aching limbs and rise to meet Mariam and Rupert. I expect them to shout from a distance, but they don't. In fact, I can tell they are raising their fingers to their mouths as if to shush us. And come to think of it, they look in a hurry, running the last few yards towards us.

Rupert has run the fastest and is out of breath, so it falls to Mariam to tell us what's going on. 'We think we can see a church spire, way over there, so that must be the village,' she whispers.

I'm just about to ask why she is being so quiet, when Rupert finds his voice. 'We can tell them about that bit later,' he hisses in urgency. 'A man is heading this way, and the vibe is not good. Like the one you described,' he pants. 'He has a gun.'

There is a split-second delay. Then Sorley and I leap to our feet and reach for our bags, pulling everything into a gap in the rock face. We duck in too – there is nothing I can do about my bright clothing now.

Oh, on reflection, there is. I pull off my red jacket and reveal a beige fleece, better than what was there before, anyway.

'Shush, Drookit,' I mumble.

Rupert carefully inches his head around the corner.

'We're in luck – he's not coming this way. He seems more interested in up there …'

We follow his pointing finger. The man stands at the foot of a sheer rockface a little way off, shelved with ledges jutting out at various angles.

'There,' Rupert whispers, pointing. 'Oh goodness!' His eyes widen. 'I get it now. Oh no … I do get what's happening now.' He swears quietly into his snood.

'What is it?' all three of us ask in urgent whispers.

Rupert raises his pointing arm to the sky.

With a piercing shriek, the huge wings of an eagle emerge from the clouds, glide over us, wide as a door and touch down high on the ledge where Rupert is pointing. New, higher noises add to the cacophony – I see two tiny heads. Of course it's hard to tell without binoculars, but basically, they look like dinosaurs with beaks. The adult eagle is carrying something – I see flashes of blood-red as well as fur. Drookit must sense our tension, for he begins to growl, first low and menacing, then guttural, louder. Mariam gives a whimper and shifts herself so that I am between her and the dog.

My brain goes fuzzy: the figure of the man is just an outline in the distance, but I see it crystal clear. The same shape, the same hunching posture. It's the older man from early in the morning. And just as the birds are feeding high above him, he raises his gun. Raises it, raises it, aims.

'He's going to shoot an eagle!' Rupert's voice cracks.

'What can we do? What can we do?'

A shot rings out, slicing through the air so painfully

that all of us flinch. The eagle, however, rises into the air with powerful wingbeats as another two shots follow.

'Is it hurt?' Mariam asks, clawing into my shoulder as she peers around it.

'Doesn't look like it. But the guy is just going to wait until the adult bird returns to feed the chicks, and he'll shoot at it again, won't he?'

The wind has turned, whipping into our faces. Drookit's growl has fizzled out – he stands stock-still, his nose twitching.

And then the makeshift leash slices into my palm as he breaks free and flies down the hill towards the stranger.

'Drookiiiiiit!'

Instead of slowing down, Bairdy's dog only speeds up on the steep slope. It won't take him all that long to reach the stranger who is already turning, and no wonder, with Drookit barking like his life depends on it. Suddenly I remember the gash in Drookit's fur, and something makes me wonder if these two have met before. *Does this man know what happened to Bairdy?*

I don't have time to articulate any of these lightning-swift thoughts. We watch in horror as the stranger swivels around and makes a loud, startled sound which the wind carries over to us. Then he points the barrel of his gun straight at Drookit, taking his time to take aim. He is not going to miss this time – not at close range.

'Noooo!' I shoot out of our hiding place. 'That's my dog!'

I half-run and half-slide down the hillside after him. 'Drookit! Stop!'

18
The Old Man

Running. Sliding. Staying on my feet – just. As I hurtle forward, I can think of nothing but Drookit, who is only a dog, and of that man who has the power to take his life away, just like that. He seems determined to do it. If Sorley, Rupert and Mariam shout after me, I don't hear it. I only hear the sliding scree as I run, stone against stone, and my heartbeat drumming in my chest. 'Drookiiiiit!'

The dog is barking, growling, agitatedly circling right and left – but he keeps his distance from the gunman who seems genuinely astonished to see me.

'Please wait! Wait sir, he means no harm,' I screech, all but throwing myself on the ground to grasp the end of Drookit's lead again. A quick glance up confirms: the adult eagle has gone. Good, at least that's something.

'What are you doing here?' the man demands. He hasn't lowered his gun.

I look around – none of the others are visible. *Think, Kenzie.*

'Erm … taking my dog for a walk?' I offer weakly.

The man narrows his eyes. Like Bairdy before, he is wearing a sort of waistcoat with a serious number of pockets, and a tweed flat cap that could be brown or green depending on how the light hits it. I am trying not to stare too hard. My guess is, he's a fair bit older than Mum, judging by his grey beard and rough voice. Brown trousers, thick boots. And, in case I forgot to mention it, a shotgun, still swinging dangerously in his hand. He looks ready to strike Drookit with the barrel in case the dog is stupid enough to come near. Drookit's growling builds to a real crescendo now, and he tugs at the lead, although I'm not stupid enough to let him go. He is baring his teeth in a threatening manner – I've not seen him do that before. Why does he hate the stranger so much?

The man has recovered his composure, and his voice sounds almost casual. 'You got lost, huh?'

I shrug. 'I'm okay.'

The man doesn't take his eyes off me. 'Been heading into the mountains all by yourself?'

I don't like lying, so I try to avoid the question. 'What's wrong with heading into the mountains by yourself?' I demand, with much more courage than I really feel.

'Don't try to pull the wool over my eyes,' he shouts, before adding more quietly: 'This is not your dog. You were not alone. Look at you, you're only a bairn. Who are you trying to kid, eh?'

My brain pieces together the clues far more slowly than I had hoped, but eventually it all clicks into place.

Drookit hates the stranger. The stranger hates Drookit. The dog had blood in his fur the night Bairdy disappeared. With every passing second, I grow more certain that the dog and the stranger have met before. This man could have been the one who injured Drookit, and that means ...

The harder I think, the more my legs turn to rubber.

How else can the stranger know that Drookit isn't my dog? Because he knows that Drookit belongs to someone else ...

I can practically feel the blood draining from my face.

My eyes travel from the dog to the stranger's shotgun. The man with all the clues about what happened to Bairdy is standing right before me. He must know what happened to our missing guide.

But I am not going to ask – not now that he has raised the barrel of the shotgun again and closed his finger around the trigger. Pointing it not at the eagle's nest, or Drookit.

No – he is pointing it straight at me.

'You better come with me, young lady. It's not safe out here on the mountain, least of all for a kid like you. Come, come, don't be shy. We'll take care of you in the lodge. Keep hold of your dog, though, or it won't go well for either of you.'

If my brain was overactive a minute ago, it goes into some sort of freeze now. I think of Mum, all by herself in

the flat. A quick glance over my shoulder confirms – my friends have not left their hiding place, though I swear I could see a flash of Rupert's jacket behind the rocks. *They are my only hope now. And I will not give them away.* I turn my head forward, grasp Drookit's lead as hard as I can and walk ahead of the armed stranger, looking resolutely ahead.

I feel numb, even though the sun begins to dip, bathing the expanse of heather in a glorious gold once more. Rustling and flutters don't delight me anymore. The man follows the circling birds above us with his eyes, mumbling scornfully under his breath. He does not try to speak to me, and I do not attempt any conversation either. Trotting along a narrow path, as we weave our way through slopes of rock and dense undergrowth alive with nesting birds, I lift my eyes to the hills. Strong. Steady. Unmoved and unruffled. *Come on Kenzie. Think!*

But however hard I try, the solution does not come to me. Then I hear a sound that is entirely out of place here – electric guitar and a drumbeat – the beginning of a song I vaguely recognise. It's a ringtone! The man behind me has stopped.

'Aha? Hi Gordy. Erm, no. Sorry, not yet. Something has come up. I'll explain once I get back to the lodge.'

I cannot make out the words, but the voice on the other end of the phone sounds angry.

'Yes ... No, I'll explain later – but this makes things a whole lot more complicated, unfortunately. No, no, don't worry, it'll be sorted. Give me another day or so, it'll be done. I'll see to it all. Never fear.'

Despite my clenched stomach and clawing fists, I can't help trying to work it out. *Explain what? Do what? See to what?*

We must have walked for an hour or more – I've lost all sense of time. Drookit is close to me, keeping to the path and mercifully, staying quiet. Eventually, in the distance, a whitewashed building rises in front of a loch. We make straight for it. Agonisingly, I think I spy a village, perhaps a mile or two along the river. I would find help there – so close now, and so out of reach. My steps slow out of fear or tiredness, I don't know which. It feels as if only half of Kenzie is here.

'Keep going. Nearly there. And then you'll have plenty of time to tell me what you were really doing up there.'

I summon all my resolve to reply. 'Why do you keep accusing me of lying? I'm just taking my dog for a walk. And okay, I may have got lost—'

'Kids don't get lost in places like that. You were up to something, and I will find out what it was before …'

He doesn't finish his sentence.

Before what?

Cold sweat forms on my neck.

BEFORE WHAT?

Drookit seems to sense my panic and nuzzles my hand. After a while, our steps crunch on unforgiving sharp gravel as we pass a gate and turn into the hunting lodge.

'Are you mad? What did you bring a kid here for?'

The voice of the younger man at dawn, I am certain

of it. He's dressed in expensive-looking tweed from top to bottom. The young gamekeeper approaches, eyeing me carefully.

'I had no choice, boss. She's only a bairn,' the older man begins, but the younger one cuts him off.

'Take her to the outbuildings and lock her in the shed – then you come in and we'll talk.'

The threat in his voice is unmistakable, and the old man feels it too. There is no point in resisting. I find myself dragged down a lane, away from the main building towards a long, low set of sheds. The younger man struts behind us, as if to make sure his instructions are followed properly. Around the corner, leaning untidily against a crumbling stone wall, lies a ragged row of fertiliser bags, just like the one they used to take the bird away on the hillside. On closer inspection, there are feathers and at times claws and beaks protruding from the bags, piled up high. *What are these?* Buzzards? Eagles? Ravens? I want to vomit. But then I feel a rough shove to my neck and find myself on my knees on the ground, inside a dark shed with a tiny window so full of cobwebs that I can barely make out anything at all.

'Wait, I hate spiders! Don't leave me here!' I scramble to my feet, accidentally yanking Drookit on his line, but the door slams shut, and I sense a heavy bar slide across. I am trapped.

'The owner and his guests are flying in tomorrow, you oaf. And they are here to collect the chicks, get it? This whole thing needs to be dealt with by then, do you hear?

Let's talk inside. We need to play this right.'

'She's only a bairn,' the old man repeats. That is the last thing I hear before the crunching of the gravel indicates their departure.

I bury my face in the dog's fur. 'Oh Drookit,' I sob and finally give my tears permission to flow.

19
The Hunting Lodge

Grandma. Mum. The school library. My room. It all feels so far away, as if it had never belonged to my life at all. Even the little I can see through the shed window tells me that the sun is dipping further – by now, it is possible, just possible that someone, somewhere will wonder why we haven't returned. Is it too late for me? I fear that it might be.

My face is crusted with tears, dust and cobwebs by the time I hear the shed door rattle – I didn't hear anyone approach! My stomach plummets. Have they decided to do away with me for good?

The bar across the door doesn't move. But it rattles a little. Then it shivers. Then it shudders. Suddenly, there is a whisper.

'Kenzie, are you in there?'

I manage to close my hand around Drookit's muzzle just in time to stop him from barking.

'Sorley? *Sorley?* Is that you?'

My voice is barely a croak.

'Yes. Mariam and Rupert are keeping watch, so help me get you out!'

'Can you move the bar?'

'I've tried – it's really stiff.'

'The window is too small,' I hiss. 'Oh, Sorley, hurry. Please hurry. They have guns and they've killed so many birds already. Did you see all the bags?'

'I did.' Sorley says no more – instead I hear him groan and strain to move the heavy bar.

'Will I kick the door?'

Sorley sounds spooked now. 'No! They'll hear. Let me just …'

I feel his whole weight against the door as he tries to force the bar open. Then a low whistle.

Sorley gasps. 'Oh no! That's the signal. They're coming.' Bile forms in my throat, but Sorley has thrown himself against the door with his full bodyweight now – and with a scrape of metal against metal, it finally gives. 'Let's go, quick quick quick!'

There is no time to run far – I drag Drookit along and we just make it behind some sort of compost heap as the men come back into view.

'You were supposed to shoot the adult eagles and bring the chicks down for the owner – you had one job! One job!' The young man's voice is impatient, and I can see him shake his head. 'Useless, so you are. You were a wimp about that meddler of a mountain guide as well. He only got what he deserved. That'll teach him not to snoop in other people's affairs or trespass on private property. If the Laird wants to hunt grouse, let him hunt grouse. Too bad that interfering toad lost his footing. Tragic. It'll be days before anyone finds him in that gully.'

The old man merely mumbles. He sounds unhappy though.

'And if you're too weak to deal with the girl, I'll do it. But don't expect to keep your job here for much longer. I don't care if you've worked here for decades. The old times have gone. I am Head Gamekeeper now, and I answer only to the new owner. And as soon as he arrives, I'll be sure to recruit a young gamekeeper who can actually follow instructions. That girl should have been down a cliff face rather than in that shed. What were you thinking?'

Sorley's face creeps near my head. 'I think we have to make a run for it,' he whispers. 'As soon as they see the shed is empty, they will look here.'

Just as well someone is thinking straight. All I am thinking of is the fact that there are still guns in these people's hands.

They turn the corner. Then the younger man swears loudly.

Both men rush towards the door of the shed, which swings on its hinge.

'NOW,' whispers Sorley, and we spring up and dart right past the open shed doorway, past the turned backs of the two men shining a torch inside. I urge Drookit on, and Sorley gives the door a heavy push as he passes, slamming hard into one or other of the men. We can hear more swearing, but not for long.

'Run in a zigzag, Kenzie!'

Gravel flies as we gallop towards the gate. Beyond it lies the small road towards the village. *Run! RUN!*

We hurtle away from the building, scramble over the gate instead of opening it, and Sorley takes a second to roll a big stone in front. Drookit wriggles through underneath and I slide the lead off him. We resume our sprint. Just as well – only the younger one is following us on foot now, thankfully running instead of aiming his gun. The older man has got into a Land Rover – the engine revs loudly. Hopefully it will take some time to get the gate open. It's the younger one we have to worry about now. *Run! RUN.*

He can only get a clear aim at us if he stops. But if he keeps running, he may gain on us. *How fit is that man? And where are Rupert and Mariam?* I didn't get a chance to ask Sorley that. The village seems light years away. I can see the lit-up windows in the distance.

In mid-run, I turn to see one of my questions answered: Mariam has emerged from a hiding place overlooking the road and is hurling stones at our pursuer. *Oh gosh, what if he turns his gun on her? And what about Rupert?*

Oh goodness, Rupert is jogging ahead of us on the road, no doubt trying to make his way to the village to raise the alarm. 'HURRY RUPERT!' I scream.

Wait. The steps of our pursuer have stopped. For a split

second I turn. Then a gunshot whizzes past my head, so close that the very air smarts. *Oh man, he is really doing this. He is shooting at kids!*

The stitch in my side intensifies and we careen around the corner. Now it's a straight, tree-lined avenue, all the way to a sign welcoming us to the village in the distance, although it's too far away to read. Sorley's gait has turned to loping, but we don't slow our pace. 'Do we ... hide in the trees?' I gasp.

'No ...' Sorley huffs back. 'Gives him ... time to ... aim. Keep going!'

He speeds up, goodness knows how. Drookit keeps up with him easily. I try to match their pace – we're gaining on Rupert who seems to be tiring now. Bushes, grasses and trees fly past us on both sides.

The engine of the Land Rover drowns out all else as it comes into view behind our pursuer. At the same time, there is a yelp as Rupert, just ahead of us, trips and crashes to the ground.

'RUPERT!'

His cry of pain is heart-splitting, even amid the rush of blood and fear in my ears. I nearly stumble over the dog as I break to a halt – the car is approaching so fast now that both Sorley and I rush to grab our injured friend and drag him from the road and out of the way. The three of us collapse in a heap on the moss by the roadside as the Land Rover shoots past us, swivels sideways and growls to a halt to block our way. The younger gunman has slowed his run to a jog, a grin spreading across his sweaty face.

Rupert whimpers in pain, but Sorley and I raise ourselves to our full height.

All out of ideas.

All out of time.

I lift my eyes up to the hills where a single eagle circles high in the sky.

All out of hope too.

20
The Pursuit

The Head Gamekeeper's tweed waistcoat hangs half open as he approaches.

'Ha! I must admit, I always suspected you weren't alone. That loathsome, interfering toad of a guide always brings young ones into these parts. We should have known there were more,' he adds over his shoulder to the older gamekeeper who has stepped out of the car.

Behind the men, I think I detect a flash of green Gore-Tex amid the trees. Sorley has seen it too. It's Mariam, sneaking past on the other side of the trees towards the village.

'What have you done with Bairdy?' shouts Sorley, despite the desperate situation we are in.

I wince – maybe letting them see that we know the worst

is not a great technique right now. But to my surprise, the younger man answers.

'Didn't do anything to him – it was the damn dog I had to worry about. Gave him a good whack with the butt of this, that's all, and then that pesky mountain guide came a bit too close to me, didn't he? Had no choice but to defend myself. Not my fault that he lost his balance …' He pauses dramatically. 'In such an unfortunate spot, too. And I didn't think it was my place to call for help or anything. After all, I barely knew the guy.' He emits a mirthless chuckle.

The old gamekeeper behind him shuffles his weight from side to side. In the distance, the eagle screeches high in the sky, as if to mock us.

The young man shrugs. 'Anyway, now we've got you. Get in the car.' He raises his gun threateningly. Sorley and I exchange a glance, but when he points the gun at Rupert, still clutching his ankle and white as a frozen puddle, we give up all hope of escape.

And then an idea strikes me. *Why didn't I think of this before?* I turn to the old man.

'Excuse me, sir. Are you on board with all of this? Wildlife crime is bad enough – killing adult birds of prey, selling eagle chicks to rich men … but murder? Do you really want to go down for the murder of three children? Is that you?'

'Shut up, pathetic little witch!' shouts the younger man, but it's working, I can see it in the old man's eyes.

'Do you have a child? Maybe you had a daughter who was just like me?'

Bullseye. There is a distinct flutter of uncertainty in the old man's eyes. His grey beard twitches. But then he roars: 'Get in the car! All of you!'

This time he presses the cold metal of his gun barrel right into Sorley's temple, so hard that it makes a circular red imprint when he moves.

'All right, all right – we're coming,' I croak hurriedly before opening the car door, slowly. Every single second gives Mariam more time. And that is all I can give her. No help, but time. *Come on Mariam!* I daren't even look up the road towards the village for fear of giving anything away. Sorley slumps, defeated. Rupert looks near to passing out, and everything about me has gone numb. The old man's mouth is a tight line, his forehead furrowed. He has wrestled with himself and made his decision, and it's not been an easy one.

I sag into the car seat like a sack of potatoes, with Drookit at my feet.

'Best to check there aren't any more, Gordy,' the old man rasps to his superior, pointing towards the trees where Mariam crouched only moments ago. 'I'll take these three and lock them in the car until you get back.'

There is something off about the way the old man doesn't look at his boss, but the younger gunman hasn't noticed.

'You'd better watch them properly this time,' he snaps before disappearing into the trees.

Our captor slides into the driver's seat, carefully places his gun at his feet, adjusts his mirror to keep a close eye on us and starts the engine, winding his window down.

'Good work,' are his parting words to his younger colleague.

Then the three of us are thrown back with unexpected force as the Land Rover's engine screams in outrage. The car spins hard and accelerates with a spray of mud and gravel. But not towards the lodge and certain doom.

No.

Towards the village, amid a startled cry from the young gunman.

'Enough,' mumbles the old man under his breath. 'Enough now.'

We hurtle past the village sign, through a red traffic light, around a corner, into a side street, across a railway track and screech to a halt beside an old-looking stone building. The sign above the double door reads Police Station and two uniformed police officers are just emerging, accompanied by the ragged looking Mariam. They freeze stock-still when our driver emerges from the car, holding his gun.

He throws his weapon to the ground, steps away from the vehicle and raises his hands. He turns to me and gives me a sad wink – something like an apology, an acknowledgement. Regret. Then he faces the officers.

'Evening, officers. I want to make a statement,' he rasps.

21
The Search

'Do you think they'll find him?' Mariam asks anxiously, chewing a large mouthful of macaroni pie.

The fire crackles in the grate in the village pub where the police left us 'to recover from our ordeal' with the chirpy landlady. She is under strict instructions to look after us in every possible way while phone calls are made to our parents.

We can't go home yet, according to the nice policewoman summoned from the nearby town – the police are not done with their investigations yet and have many more questions for us. Sorley's camera film has to be developed in a hurry, and Mariam needs to give her statement about what she saw when the men threatened us. Both the old gamekeeper and his younger boss were taken away in a police van earlier, and we watched anxiously from the window of our room upstairs as a mountain rescue team in high visibility jackets assembled outside. Rupert was a good help to them, using both his compass and his map to pinpoint the rough area where our guide went missing. After questioning us all, the mountain rescue leader narrowed the options down to a few gullies. 'Still a big area, but with this information there may be a chance, even after all this time.' With that, he rose to set off with his team, speaking into a crackling walkie-talkie.

Soon, we hear a coastguard helicopter thunder overhead, rising like a giant dragonfly towards the peaks.

'The coastguard helicopters have amazing camera equipment to search this kind of landscape,' Ruperts says. 'They even have winches for dropping search volunteers off or lifting injured people. I really hope they find him,' he adds.

There is a strained silence – of worry and exhaustion and not a little disbelief that we are really sitting here in the warmth, tucking into pub food. My lasagne is easily the best thing I have ever eaten. Only when I think of Bairdy does my stomach knot.

'Hard to think that we came down from all the way up there.'

'Especially me,' comments Sorley drily and we chuckle, but it is a heavy laugh. The weight of the last two days pulls at my eyelids.

In the distance we see the torches of the rescue team, moving jerkily in the dusk. Thankfully, an almost full moon

is set to rise, which will help the rescue effort. If conditions are too challenging and it gets too dark, the search will be called off until tomorrow, I heard the mountain rescue leader say.

'I'm glad they took Drookit,' Sorley speaks into the silence as we try and fail to keep the worst outcomes out of our imaginations. 'If anyone can find Bairdy, it's his own dog.'

We watch as the hands of the clock above the pub fireplace move slowly. Five past nine. Ten past nine. The remains of my lasagne (it was good, but I just can't finish an adult portion) have long gone cold and the landlady collects the plates. Half past nine.

'I think they're coming back,' says Rupert, pointing his miniature binoculars at the dull panes of the pub window. Darkness has settled like a cloak outside, but yes, in the distance the little lights dance towards us once more while the coastguard helicopter zooms overhead and disappears northeast, back towards its base. Whenever the moon emerges from the clouds, it bathes the mountains in a ghostly milk-white light, reflected by thousands of hidden pools and puddles. Places where the *Sìdh* roam – if the stories are to be believed.

My heart sinks. *Have they given up already? But what if he is still alive?* Frustration boils up inside me. If I'm honest, it's not just fear for our guide's safety – after all, we only met him three days ago. It is also about the missing pieces of the jigsaw. What did he see? What really happened to him?

A familiar battered minibus screeches into the car park, and a young blonde woman I recognise from the day we set off jumps out. Moments later she crashes through the pub doors.

'Sorry, no new orders now,' begins the landlady before making the connection. 'Ah, are you here because of the incident?'

The woman ignores the question and breathlessly leaps into questions of her own. 'Have they found him? The missing man, Ivor Baird? He's my colleague. My friend. My …' Her eyes well up. She doesn't finish her sentence, and it's clear she cares for our mountain guide, maybe more than she realised herself. Suddenly it strikes me how alone she is as she stands there, how much like a child herself, how helpless. I rise.

'Hi. I'm Kenzie. We were Bairdy's group up there, until he went missing. Come, sit with us. What's your name?'

Mariam fetches some napkins from the counter while I guide the woman called Meg towards an empty seat by our table. The boys pat her awkwardly on the back as she dabs her eyes.

Finally, Rupert cracks under the awkward silence. 'Well, we think the rescue team are going to be back any m—'

He is interrupted by the creak of the door. Weary footsteps drag across the hallway. Our heads swivel round, all hints of tiredness gone.

The leader of the rescue team enters first. His expression is unreadable. Behind him, two volunteers enter at once, carrying between them a stretcher. On it lies a limp and familiar body. I look away before forcing myself to look again: Bairdy's face is grey, scratched and swollen, and his trousers torn. His ankle points away from his leg at an angle that turns my stomach. I'd be convinced he was dead if it wasn't for the unearthly groan passing through his gritted teeth.

The woman beside us stares, motionless. Then she springs up and flies at him. 'BAIRDY!'

Bairdy's next groan turns into her name, but the rescue leader stops her from hugging the injured man. 'Whoa, easy, easy! This one will need painkillers right away, and a doctor, and then a good rest too. The air ambulance is on its way; that field beside the pub is big enough for it to land. Gentle now!'

The landlady ushers us away to 'give them some privacy' as once again the rumbling of a helicopter approaches, and Bairdy is carried at speed to the waiting air ambulance. The woman goes with him and moments later, they are airborne, northbound for the hospital in Inverness where Bairdy's injuries are going to be checked out and his fractures can be set properly.

All the rest of it happens in a dream. Mum arrives and hugs me so hard that I think I will have to join Bairdy in hospital with a bunch of broken ribs. Sorley's, Mariam's and Rupert's folks appear too, and all the parents talk to each other. I hear everything as if underwater. We gather our things and our parents make appointments with our local police stations where we will be interviewed some more.

And all the while, the mountains stand guard around us, pointing skywards to freedom and adventure, and I am confused because I do not know what to feel anymore.

As soon as I sink into the passenger seat of Mum's battered Fiat, I allow sleep to claim me.

Bairdy, Drookit, and the four of us. *Am Fear Liath Mòr*, the Cuth's announcements and the spectre of secondary school after the summer mingle into a swirling stream of images and sounds and feelings. I lose track of what is real and what is not.

And perhaps it does not matter.

22
The New Normal

'Right, that's it! No more talking, do you hear, and less of your cheek, Sorley Mackay. Get up and move seats! Over here at the front, beside Kenzie please.'

Claudia and her posse snicker in the back row. Of course, it hasn't taken Sorley long to build up a reputation for troublemaking at our new secondary school, and no one objects to him more than Mr. Dawkins, our geography teacher. He thinks that forcing Sorley to sit beside me is a terrible punishment, but as soon as he arrives, my pal gives me a secret wink. We don't hang out all the time – he has his own group of friends, and I have Mariam. But we are a team. The mountains have seen to that.

'Talk at lunchtime,' he whispers.

I look at my watch. Forty-seven minutes until outdoors

club – my favourite time of the week.

'Yeah! Can't wait for the trip next month!' I whisper back enthusiastically.

Too enthusiastically, it turns out.

'Kenzie! That's enough. I moved Sorley to the front so he would work, not for you to start talking, too.' Our geography teacher sounds exasperated.

'Sorry Sir,' I say dutifully, with only the tiniest hint of rebellious sarcasm. Mariam elbows me from the other side. Fair enough – probably best to get my head down and work on our weather forecasts before we all get reported to the year head.

Secondary school hasn't been the nightmare I anticipated. Far from it, in fact. It turns out that most of the teachers are impressed by a girl who uses big words and loves to learn more of them. Plus, there are so many clubs and activities – I can't even keep count. I volunteered for library duty straight away, and not only was I issued with a classy lanyard with a badge that says *Reading Rocks* in swirly writing, but I also get out of class for things like author visits and book fairs. *Stop daydreaming, Kenzie! Now focus on the names of these clouds!* For someone who likes big words, I am having trouble remembering all these Latin terms: cumulus, stratus and nimbus. Or was that cirrus? Oh, I don't know!

At long last, the bell rings. Most of our class crash through the door as soon as we are dismissed to be first in line for school dinners. Not us. Not Rupert, Sorley, Mariam and me.

We bring a packed lunch on Fridays because we wouldn't dream of missing a single minute of Friday lunchtime – especially not this week when our club will welcome a special visitor. The science department is already crowded with pupils and eventually the biology teacher who heads up the club lets us into her classroom.

'BAIRDY!' The four of us rush forward towards the teacher's desk, only to stop again, a little awkwardly. When we suggested him as a possible guest speaker for the club, I hadn't thought about how it would feel to see him after all this time. A quick sideways glance at Mariam, Sorley and Rupert confirms that they feel the same: a little awkward, a little embarrassed.

Bairdy, on the other hand, seems unencumbered by any of that. 'Oh, come here, the four of you!' he roars before enfolding us in a rib-crushing, breath-stopping hug. 'Ow,' he winces immediately and lets go. 'I guess those fractures haven't quite healed yet!'

'You started it!' Sorley counters and we all laugh. The story of our trip to the hills has become legend in the school already and everybody else watches Bairdy with a mixture of awe, suspicion and morbid fascination.

'Don't worry! I'm all right, nothing to see here.' He waves the concerned faces away. 'But thanks for getting your teacher to make contact. Being a volunteer for your club is exactly what I need – something positive to do while I wait for these bones to heal and for the trial to finish. I'd be going round the bend without Meg keeping me company when she can. She's been great.'

'Okay, stop staring at our guest, everyone,' the science teacher adds, tying her dark hair into a ponytail. 'All of you, grab a seat and have some lunch – then we can agree on our activities for the next few weeks, including our expedition, before Ivor Baird tells us about his career as a mountain guide. And Ivor, thanks for coming into school, we really appreciate it. Maybe you'd like to sit with your young friends as we eat? Do you want me to move your bag?'

Bairdy pats the large holdall at his feet. 'No, it's fine here, thanks.'

It's seriously wonderful to see Bairdy like this again. We never got a chance to speak to him after our ordeal – he was whisked away to hospital, and we travelled home where we had to assist the police with their enquiries and record our evidence interviews. Sorley, attention-seeker that he is, makes Bairdy give the whole classroom a blow-by-blow account of his encounter with the criminals. I barely breathe when he describes filming the gamekeepers on his phone camera. The young gamekeeper wrestled it off him and shoved him so hard that Bairdy lost his balance and went over the cliff-edge. I don't know how Bairdy can recall the experience so calmly; I am sweating just thinking about it. He finishes matter-of-factly: 'The young guy tried to erase my footage, but the police found my phone in the lodge and recovered the video file from its deleted folder. Thank goodness I recorded it all, the whole thing. As far as my accident is concerned …'

'It wasn't exactly an accident,' mumbles Rupert.

'Fine. As far as my fall is concerned, I would not be

alive if it hadn't been for the four of you. The very least I can do is help out at your outdoors club, right?'

'So, what's the latest with the trial?' I ask.

'These things can take a while. But they've both pleaded guilty, thank goodness, so that will help,' Bairdy explains. 'The young man will get prison time, there's no doubt about that. But the old gamekeeper was the one who came forward of his own account, so the judge may be more lenient with him. I hope so. He wrote to me, you know? To apologise for not standing up to his boss when he knew they were doing wrong.'

We catch Bairdy up with what we've done in the outdoors club so far: scattering bee bombs of wildflower seed on the slopes around the school, making bird feeders for winter, planting some native shrubs donated by the local garden centre by the entrance of the school.

'And now you want to get into the hills again?' Bairdy asks. 'Meg and I could take you.'

The biology teacher nods with feeling – she has lots of rewilding posters up on her wall, so I reckon they'll all get on like a house on fire.

'Then let's start planning! I'm buzzing,' he grins, spreading a large map over two tables and pulling a notebook from his back pocket.

Something catches the corner of my vision. 'Erm Bairdy – did your bag just move?'

He leans over to unzip the holdall.

'Drookit!' Mariam and I exclaim, rushing forward to bury our faces in our friend's fur.

'Not scared anymore then, huh Mariam?' Bairdy smiles. 'I know I'm not supposed to bring him in here, but I couldn't very well leave him, could I?'

'You're the worst!' Sorley declares in a comedy telling-off voice, and everyone laughs, even the teacher.

23
Into the Hills

I tighten the belt of my backpack and clip it into place over my hips. It's not shiny and clean anymore – it proudly bears the scars of that night on the hills when my friends left it behind with all of their things as they followed me and the old gamekeeper. It hasn't done it any harm though. If anything, the pack has become part of me, just like the red waterproof jacket has become as good as a second skin. We're ahead of most of our club, dawdling behind us in an ever-contracting and unravelling chain of people, with Bairdy's girlfriend and our teacher bringing up the rear. Rowan trees bend their branches, heavy with berries.

'Folk believed these trees would protect you against *Sìdh* magic. Oh, look over there! Stop, guys.' Bairdy doesn't have to shout – we agreed on a hand signal to prompt us all to pay attention. He motions at a rock some way off. In the morning sun, an adder is sunning itself. We wait until everyone is gathered around us.

'See it, over there? That's the only venomous snake in the British Isles,' Bairdy explains. 'Isn't it a beauty? Gotta leave it alone and it will do the same for you.'

Picking up the pace, we resume our walk upwards on the narrow path, leaving the stream behind in the glen below. Just like last time, Bairdy points out a bunch of plants and flowers – although they are different from the spring ones now that we have reached September. I soak up the new words thirstily and repeat them quietly under my breath. Knapweed. Bog Asphodel. Harebell, which looks just like a bluebell to me. Grass-of-Parnassus and the best name ever, Devil's-bit Scabious. From time to time, Bairdy calls out 'eyes to the skies' which seems to be his new favourite phrase. I'm not even too much out of breath as we stop for the evening and set up camp – only one overnight this time. Drookit circles around us as if he's casting a protective dog-spell.

To protect us from what? The Grey Man? The Sìdh? I don't even know.

But I do know that I prefer the song of the skylarks to any music I have heard before or since. And as we sink to the ground for another storytelling session over hot chocolate and marshmallows, I reflect on the faces I see around me, framed by a chain of more and more familiar peaks. I barely remember the old Kenzie of five months ago.

The new Kenzie doesn't mind strangers too much anymore.

My eyes meet Mariam's. Drookit has snuggled in under Sorley's arm as Mariam pats the dog cautiously from the other side. Rupert passes me a biscuit. Yes, this new Kenzie definitely does friends. And perhaps I am in my natural habitat after all.

The last of the blooming heather prickles through my trousers and the grasses sway in the wind. I lift my eyes to where the rocky peaks are dipped in amber gold, and the air is full of song and brilliance and adventure.

THE END

Author's Note

I lift up my eyes to the mountains—where does my help come from? (Psalm 121:1)

I vividly remember my first hill walk in Scotland. The Pap of Glencoe, or *Sgorr na Cich*e to give it its proper name, is one of the most iconic and familiar landmarks in the Highlands. As someone who is uneasy with heights, I loved the sense of achievement as we finally reached the top. It was a little cloudy, but we took endless group photos by the cairn anyway. It was so much more than a walk – aside from spending a few hours surrounded by spectacular views, it was about being together and making memories with friends. Come to think of it, that is what draws me to the wilderness still.

But let's be honest, I am far from hardcore mountaineering material – about as far removed as you can get from the muscular, sinewy, weatherbeaten and daring Bairdy-type. Therefore, my gut reaction when Rob Lovell of the Scottish Mountaineering Press approached me about a collaboration was thinly veiled panic.

I needn't have worried. They were looking for an accessible adventure, which just happened to be set in the Scottish mountains. The kind of story which showed that the hills are for everyone. They needed a storyteller.

I thought about it. *This,* I reflected, *may be something I could do.*

But it isn't just my story. Rob Lovell's strong belief in the story from the start was invaluable – he loves the mountains and knows so much about the environment I was trying to evoke. Thanks, too, to Helen Sedgwick for her perceptive editing and kind words of encouragement, to Lorenne Brogan for her eagle-eyed error-spotting and to illustrator Victoria Holt and designer Gino Di Meo for their gorgeous work. In addition, I am grateful to my experts: Alan Hepburn, teacher and trustee of the rewilding charity *Scotland: The Big Picture*, for his thoughts on rewilding and land management – Bairdy's strong views owe a lot to my conversation with him. I am also indebted to Raghnaid Sandilands, a creative ethnologist, Gaelic translator, map maker, writer and publisher who recommended Mollie Hunter's *The Haunted Mountain* to me whilst pointing me to other Gaelic Folklore sources. I am also hugely indebted to Ruth Tingay of Raptor Persecution UK for her expertise and generosity. In the interest of balance, it is important to recognise that, of course, most gamekeepers have chosen to spend their working lives outdoors because they love nature. However, at times, responsible gamekeepers may come under pressure to do things which may be illegal.

And finally, thanks to Conor Cromie of the Cairngorm Mountain Rescue Team, as well as Fiona, Helen and Ross of Mountaineering Scotland, for their expertise and generosity. This book is much better for their input, and any remaining errors are my own.

What do I hope this story will achieve? I dare to hope that young story lovers will visit the hills in their imaginations.

And maybe, just maybe, it will make them want to have their own adventures.

After all, the hills are for everyone.

Want to know more? Here are some extra bits!

ENJOYING THE GREAT OUTDOORS IN SCOTLAND

You should always...
- Respect the interests of other people.
- Care for the environment.
- Take responsibility for your own actions.

Here are some good principles...
- If camping, use small tents and camp well away from buildings, roads and farmland – and have a backup plan to go somewhere else if it's busy.
- Do not light an open fire, including in fire bowls or BBQs, during times of high fire risk (prolonged periods of dry weather) or near forests, farmland, peaty

ground, or close to buildings or historic sites. Always pay attention to fire danger warnings and report any out-of-control fires you find by calling 999 immediately.

- If you need to, use a camping stove to cook your food. Place it on a level, non-flammable surface away from dry grass and vegetation (and your tent!) and keep a close watch while using it.
- Take away all belongings and litter and leave no trace of your visit. When cleaning up, pick up any pieces of broken glass with the rest of your rubbish, as these act as a magnifying glass for the sun and can start fires.
- Remember that deadwood provides a home and food for many creatures and is vital for the ecosystem. So, leave the wood on the ground and never cut down or damage trees.
- Prepare for the call of nature. If there aren't public toilets nearby, pack a trowel, toilet paper, hand sanitiser, and sealable bags for your litter to make it easy to clean up. Wash your hands with water or use hand sanitiser afterwards.

Check these out...

 Scan this to find out more about camping in Scotland at the **Scottish Outdoor Access Code** website.

 Scan this to read about staying healthy when you're outdoors at the **Mountaineering Scotland** website.

BEING PREPARED FOR THE HILLS (AND EVERYTHING THEY MIGHT THROW AT YOU!)

Bringing the right kit is one of the most important ways to keep yourself safe in the hills. Here are some things to think about:

The kit you need will depend a lot on the type of activity you are planning, and what the conditions will be like. If you are unsure, just ask for advice in a reputable outdoor shop. As a general rule of thumb, you should think about the following for a hillwalking trip.

Footwear
You will need well-fitting walking boots and comfortable socks.

Clothing
It's always a good idea to opt for layers as this keeps you flexible. Man-made fibres are better than cotton t-shirts or jeans which absorb and retain moisture and can get heavy and wet, or chafe. A breathable, waterproof jacket with a hood is a must, ideally in a bright colour so you can be spotted easily should things go wrong.

Bag
Bring a waterproof rucksack (or a waterproof cover for it), but make sure the bag is no bigger than what you need for the trip. You don't want to expend needless energy.

Food and Drink

Arguably, the best part of the day is eating sandwiches at the summit! Don't forget that going out into the hills uses a lot of energy, so be sure to pack enough food for your adventure. Sweets are great for an energy boost when you are feeling tired, but also include something that will power you for a bit longer – a nice cheese sandwich, for example. You should have enough food for the whole of your journey, plus a little extra as emergency supplies. Always carry a water bottle.

Other Essentials

These depend on the weather – a sun hat, sunglasses and sunscreen along with midge repellent/net will be important in summer. A head torch, map and compass, mobile phone and group shelter should also be carried, just in case you get into trouble or end up being out longer than you expect.

Check these out...

Scan this to get more advice on staying safe in the hills from the **Scottish Mountain Rescue** website.

Scan this to get more info on all the essential kit you'll need at the **Mountaineering Scotland** website.

HOW DOES IT WORK?
NAVIGATING WITH A COMPASS

You may not even be sure what a compass is! Well, it is a tool for hillwalkers which points out directions: North, South, East and West. If you want to impress your teacher or your parents, you can casually call these 'cardinal directions'.

Each compass contains a needle, which is a piece of magnetised metal that points towards the Earth's magnetic North Pole. A pocket compass is portable and user-friendly, almost like a watch. If you hold it in your hand, it will point in a northern direction.

You probably already know that the Earth is a huge magnet with two centres of force known as the North and South Poles. The core of our Earth, containing molten metal, spins around, creating a magnetic field with the north and south magnetic poles at either end. If this wasn't the case, compasses would not work.

The needle is balanced on a pin, and covered in liquid so it can freely turn. All you need to do is hold the compass flat and level on your hand, and the needle will detect the Magnetic North and point to it.

When combined with detailed maps (the most commonly used being those from Ordnance Survey), a compass becomes a powerful tool for navigating in the mountains. With a map, compass and a simple way to measure distance like counting your paces, it's possible to navigate in almost zero visibility!

A great place to start learning some of these techniques

is by going orienteering, and you should be able to find local orienteering clubs by searching online.

Check these out...

 Scan this for more info on map reading and using a compass at **BBC Bitesize**.

 Scan this to find more skills that you need to find your way around the hills at the **Mountaineering Scotland** website.

HELP! EMERGENCY!

Let's be clear – only a very small proportion of those heading to the hills get into serious difficulty. However, with the best will in the world, things can sometimes go wrong. Here are some good principles for keeping yourself and others safe whilst enjoying the outdoors:

Before you set out, it is always a good idea to let a responsible person know the details of where you are going, what you are doing and when you plan to be back before you leave. Checking a mountain-specific weather forecast is also crucial, and in winter you must be sure to research snow conditions and avalanche risks for your chosen area.

If you or someone in your group has an accident, the first rule is to stay calm, consider your situation and work out what to do next.

Get yourself and others out of immediate danger and use your first aid kit to help anyone injured. You will then need to decide: Can you get down from the hills safely yourself? Do you need shelter? Do you need to stay put, or call for help?

If you call for help in the mountains, call 999 or 112, ask for the Police and then ask for Mountain Rescue. They will want to know where you are (as exact as possible), how many people are with you and the nature of their injuries.

Scottish Mountain Rescue is a great charity and will respond at any hour, on any day and in any weather. Their highly trained volunteers carry out a specialist search and rescue service (often with the help of helicopters with all sorts of cool technology) in the mountains and remote communities in Scotland. Their aim is to help people if and when they get into difficulty. In short, they save lives. Why not consider a fundraiser for their crucial work?

First Aid

If you head into the hills, you should always carry a first aid kit in case of injury. This should contain at least the following items:

- Plasters, dressings and bandages
- Tape, scissors and safety pins
- Antiseptic wipes
- Tweezers and tick-twisters
- Pain relief, e.g. paracetamol or ibuprofen
- Hand sanitiser
- Instant ice pack for treating sprains etc.
- Wound closure strips
- Foil survival blanket
- First aid information booklet

One last thing!

Scan this for **The St John's Ambulance** website. They have great resources and videos on first aid. You can also download their free first aid app. It is so much better to be prepared than be caught out in a crisis.

Register your mobile phone with the 999 text service in case the signal in your location is too weak to support a call – it still may be enough for a text message. Scan this to find out more at **Mountaineering Scotland**.

GAELIC FOLKLORE AND THE MOUNTAINS

Scotland is a country rich in stories – perhaps the weather lends itself to storytelling around the hearth. Ballads and songs about Scotland's landscape, its heroes and battles abound, but so do stories about the supernatural: ghosts, monsters and magical creatures.

References to these can often be found in the naming of features in the landscape – look out for hills with the word *Sìdh* in them, which are places where the fairy folk were said to have dwelt. The Munro Schiehallion (an English derivation of Sìdh Chailleann, Fairy Hill of the Caledonians), is perhaps one of the most well-known examples of this.

There are just too many stories to include here, so we thought we would point you to some books and resources instead:

Books
- *An Illustrated Treasury of Scottish Folk and Fairy Tales*, Theresa Breslin, illustrated by Kate Leiper
- *An Illustrated Treasury of Scottish Mythical Creatures*, Theresa Breslin, illustrated by Kate Leiper
- *Scottish Fairy Tales, Myths and Legends*, Mairi Kidd
- *The Haunted Mountain*, Mollie Hunter

Check out these websites...

 Scan this for more about myths, folklore and legends at **Scotland.org**.

 Scan this to read about the folklore of the Cairngorms at **visitcairngorms.com**.

 Scan this to visit **folklorescotland.com,** a whole website about the folklore of Scotalnd.

RAPTOR PERSECUTION

I Don't Do Mountains presents raptor persecution as one of the issues facing the Scottish outdoors. It's a subject people are worried about because these birds are important to biodiversity and need to be protected. While raptor persecution sometimes happens in places where land is managed for activities like grouse shooting, it's important to remember that this isn't always the case. Many estates look after wildlife, and help with conservation to protect these amazing birds. To address raptor persecution, people need to work together to make sure birds of prey are safe and can thrive.

 Scan this to find out more about wildlife crime from the **Royal Society for the Protection of Birds**.

All profits from Scottish Mountaineering Press books
go to help fund the Scottish Mountaineering Trust,
a Scottish charity that provides grants to projects and
organisations that promote recreation, knowledge and safety
in the mountains, especially the mountains of Scotland.

www.thesmt.org.uk